Good Neighbors?

The United States and Latin America

Ann E. Weiss

Houghton Mifflin Company
Boston 1985

For Rebecca

Library of Congress Cataloging in Publication Data

Weiss, Ann E., 1943–
  Good neighbors?

  Bibliography: p.
  Includes index.
  Summary: A history of the relationship between the United States and Latin America.
    1. Latin America—Foreign relations—United States—Juvenile literature.   2. United States—Foreign relations —Latin America—Juvenile literature.   [1. Latin America— Foreign relations—United States.   2. United States— Foreign relations—Latin America]   I. Title.
  F1418.W3   1985   327.7308   85-14383
  ISBN 0-395-36316-0

Printed in the United States of America

Q 10 9 8 7 6 5 4 3 2 1

Contents

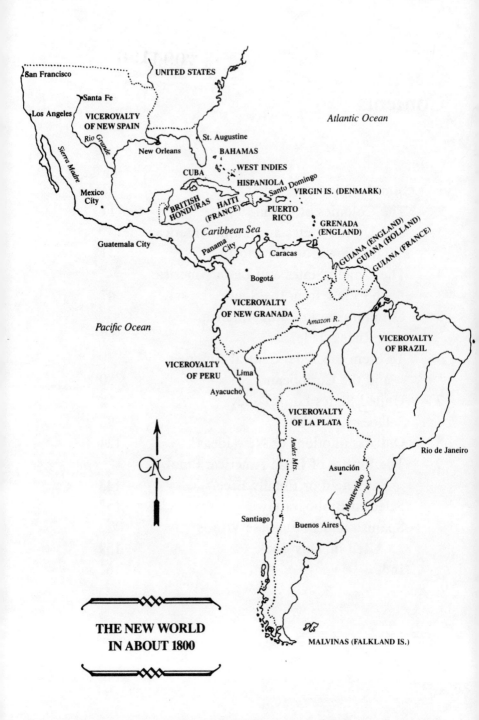

THE NEW WORLD
IN ABOUT 1800

UNITED STATES

Atlantic Ocean

Rio Grande

MEXICO

Mexico City

Sierra Madre

BAHAMAS

CUBA

WEST INDIES

DOMINICAN REPUBLIC

JAMAICA

PUERTO RICO (U.S.)

VIRGIN IS. (U.S.)

BELIZE

HONDURAS

HAITI

Caribbean Sea

GUATEMALA

EL SALVADOR

NICARAGUA

COSTA RICA

PANAMA

GRENADA

TRINIDAD

TOBAGO

GUYANA

SURINAM

FRENCH GUIANA

VENEZUELA

CONTADORA I.

COLOMBIA

Pacific Ocean

ECUADOR

Quito

Amazon R.

BRAZIL

PERU

Lima

Brasília

Andes Mts.

La Paz

BOLIVIA

São Paulo

Rio de Janeiro

PARA-GUAY

Asun-ción

CHILE

ARGENTINA

Santiago

Buenos Aires

Montevideo

URUGUAY

N

MALVINAS (FALKLAND IS.)

MODERN LATIN AMERICA

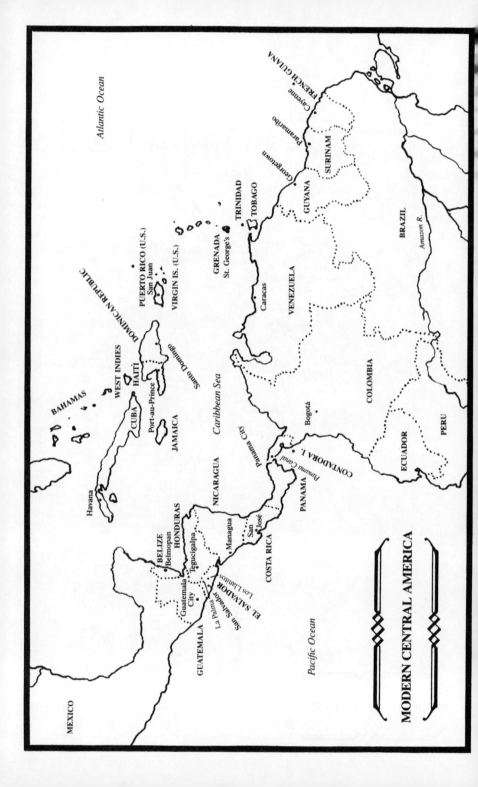

MODERN CENTRAL AMERICA

Good Neighbors?

1
Simple Questions?

"The simple questions are:

"Will we support freedom in this hemisphere or not?

"Will we defend our vital interests in this hemisphere or not?

"Will we stop the spread of communism in this hemisphere or not?

"Will we act while there is still time?"

The speaker's soft, pleasant voice rang with quiet concern. Earnestly, he leaned forward, gazing into the television cameras, challenging his listeners. For this man was asking no idle questions. He was sounding a warning, a call to battle. President Ronald Reagan was summoning the Congress and the people of the United States to join him in a fight to "protect" the nations of Latin America from "the threat of communist aggression and subversion." The day was May 9, 1984, and the president was broadcasting his appeal coast-to-coast.

As President Reagan outlined it, the situation in

Latin America certainly sounded perilous. The island of Cuba, only ninety miles from the U.S. mainland, is already a communist nation. It has been one since Fidel Castro seized power there in 1959. Soon after Castro became premier, Cuba began receiving aid from the Soviet Union. Loans and gifts of money, military equipment, and technological advice all flooded in. Before long, Cuba had become a firm ally of the communist superpower.

Of course, Cuba itself is a small nation, one that cannot threaten the United States directly. But the fact that Soviet technicians and military personnel live and work in Cuba could be a problem. The Soviets have built sophisticated military bases on the island. What if they were to use those bases from which to launch an attack on the United States?

Nor is the "communist reign of terror" limited to Cuba, President Reagan declared. Painstakingly, he described how the Cuban government urges people in other parts of Latin America to rebel against governments that are noncommunist or pro–United States.

The government of the Central American nation of Nicaragua, for instance, used to be a staunch ally of the United States. In the late 1970s, Nicaraguan rebels began attacking that government. At first the attacks failed, President Reagan said. Then, he went on, the rebels were summoned to Cuba, "where Castro cynically instructed them in the ways of successful communist insurrection." In 1979, those rebels seized power and Nicaragua became a communist state.

Like Cuba, Nicaragua established ties with the Soviet Union. That could mean, President Reagan warned, "communist military bases on the mainland of this hemisphere and communist subversion spreading southward and northward."

Actually, the subversion was already spreading, the president continued. Northwest of Nicaragua is the nation of El Salvador. El Salvador has been working to establish and maintain a democratic form of government. But that government was under attack from rebels, rebels who were, according to Reagan, armed, trained, and led by military experts from both Nicaragua and Cuba.

Communists and members of other socialist or left-wing groups have been active elsewhere in Central America and in the island nations of the Caribbean Sea. In Guatemala, the northernmost nation of Central America, small bands of terrorists were launching antigovernment attacks, then fleeing back to hide-outs in the mountains. Rebels in Honduras were following the same guerrilla tactics. Panama, at the extreme southern end of Central America, has had its own communists. So have such Caribbean nations as Grenada and the Dominican Republic.

All the communist activity boded ill for Latin American freedom, President Reagan told the nation. El Salvador was in real danger of falling to communism. Honduras, Guatemala, and Panama might fall, too, like a series of unsteadily balanced dominoes toppling over at the slightest touch. Then what hope would there be for the remaining "dominoes" of Central America: Belize and Costa Rica? What hope for the Caribbean islands? And with Central America and the Caribbean under the sway of communism, how long could South America remain free of it? To President Reagan, looking intently into the cameras as he addressed the nation, the logic of the "domino theory" was inescapable. Central America, he said, "has become the stage for a bold attempt by the Soviet Union, Cuba, and Nicaragua to install communism by force throughout the hemisphere."

Throughout the hemisphere. Does that mean that the threat to Central America is a threat to North America — including the United States — as well? President Reagan thought so. "America's economy and well-being are at stake," he said. By "America," the president meant the United States of America. If Central America cannot defend its freedom against communism, he went on, "the risks to our security and our way of life will be infinitely greater."

It was, the president said, to try to reduce those risks that he was appearing on television that May evening. He asked Congress to vote to spend more money on military aid to Central America. The increases would have to be substantial to do any good, the president added. The United States needed to double or even triple what it was already spending there.

Some of the money would go to help the Salvadoran army defeat that nation's leftist revolutionaries. Even as the president spoke, the United States was spending millions to equip and train the Salvadorans. This was helping the anticommunist effort, Reagan said. But more needed to be done.

Other funds would be used in Nicaragua. Naturally, they would not go to the communist government there. Instead, the money would be spent to help anticommunist rebels who were fighting against that government.

Much United States aid to the Nicaraguan rebels has been supplied through this country's Central Intelligence Agency (CIA). Undercover CIA agents have provided the anticommunists with money, arms, and training. They have helped groups of rebels organize attacks on such government facilities as oil storage depots and electric power stations. The aid has been useful, the president said. But, as in El Salvador, much more was needed.

More would be needed in other parts of Central America as well, Reagan warned. Guatemala, Honduras, and Panama had to build up their military strength if they were to withstand communist pressure. Belize and Costa Rica, which had only small, weak military or police forces in 1984, needed to be encouraged to develop stronger ones. A communist attack could come in either country at any time.

In his speech, President Reagan spoke mostly of communism in Central America. He referred only indirectly to the nations of South America. Those watching and listening to him, however, had no doubt that he would be quick to ask for aid for that continent, too, if communist movements there became more active.

But would he get that aid if he asked for it? And would he get the Central American aid he was asking for now? Despite his eloquence, President Reagan was having trouble convincing Congress and the people that the United States was following the right policy in Latin America.

One issue that troubled many in this country concerned CIA actions in Nicaragua. Some of the things that agency has done to help the anticommunist rebels there are illegal under international law. Nations around the world have condemned certain CIA methods as acts of war.

War — that was another matter that bothered many. If the United States continued military assistance to Central American anticommunists, might U.S. soldiers one day find themselves fighting and dying in the rugged mountains and thick jungles of Latin America? All the signs indicated that that could happen. The amount of U.S. money being spent in Central America was growing. The intensity of the fighting was increasing. El Salvador's need for U.S. help seemed to be increasing, too. If the United States did become involved in a major war in Latin America, it would most likely find that the communists it was fighting against were supported by — perhaps armed and supplied by — the Soviet Union. Could U.S. support for anticommunists in Central America escalate into all-out war between the two superpowers? Into a nuclear war?

Another question raised by many who opposed U.S. policy in Central America was this: What was the United States working *for* there? Everyone knew what the United States was *against* — the economic system known as communism. In a strictly communist country, the government controls every aspect of business and moneymaking. Individuals are not permitted to own and run private enterprises, as they are in the United States. In addition, communist nations are often political dictatorships. Freedom of religion, speech, and the press — freedoms that people in a democracy like the United States take for granted — are rare under a communist government.

But what about the anticommunist governments that the United States supports in Latin America? What are they like?

In many cases, not very admirable. Nearly all of Latin America's right-wing anticommunist governments have been as undemocratic as any communist government could be.

The government of El Salvador is an example. True, in 1984, that country elected a new president. He seemed to be trying to run his nation in a democratic way. Many, however, wondered if he could succeed.

In El Salvador, as in most of the other nations of Latin America, civilian politicians are overshadowed by the military. A nonmilitary person may be president, but army officers hold the real reins of power. Usually, they exercise that power brutally — kidnapping, torturing, and murdering anyone who speaks out against them. That has been the case in El Salvador. Between 1979 and 1984, forty thousand Salvadoran men, women, and children may have died at the hands of the government's army and police. Yet it was into these hands that President Reagan was eager to put more United States military and economic aid.

It is much the same story in other Central American nations. President Reagan asked for more funds for Panama, Honduras, and Guatemala. At the time, all three were controlled, directly or indirectly, by the military. Of the seven countries of Central America, only Costa Rica and Belize enjoyed real democratic governments in 1984. But the United States was trying to persuade those nations to build up powerful military organizations. If they do, will their democratic institutions survive?

Finally, many in the United States believe that we need to take a closer look at what is behind communist and other leftist rebel activity in Latin America. We need to know not just that such activity takes place but why it takes place.

The conditions under which most Latin Americans spend their lives are appalling by U.S. standards. A few Latin Americans are very rich, but millions live in poverty so extreme that most of us cannot even imagine it. In some countries, nearly half the population cannot find work. At the same time, prices are soaring, and the basic necessities of life are growing scarcer. Populations are increasing at a rapid rate. That suggests that future unemployment and shortages may be even worse. Millions of Latin Americans lack decent housing. They receive little or no health care. Their governments are generally harsh and often corrupt. "From the time they wake up in the morning, life is a struggle," says Father Adrian Carvery, a Roman Catholic priest who lives and works in Central America.

Is it the daily struggle to survive that makes Latin America seethe with unrest? Or was President Reagan correct when he blamed all rebel activity on prodding by communist nations such as Cuba, Nicaragua, and the Soviet Union? Or is the unrest the result of some complex mixture of both — and of other factors as well? These are not simple questions, but complicated and difficult ones. Many in the United States believe we should try to find some answers to them before we continue with our present policies in Latin America.

Yet if the United States does abandon its current policy, it will be abandoning the policy of nearly two centuries. Ronald Reagan was not the first president to believe that this country has a right — even a moral obligation — to assist Latin Americans in running their countries. The pattern of United States intervention in Latin affairs goes back to the very beginnings of independence in the Western Hemisphere.

It is a pattern that some foresaw even then. One who warned of it was the great South American freedom fighter Simón Bolívar. Early in the nineteenth century, Bolívar helped lead his land to freedom from rule by Spain. Yet as he did so, he sensed that the years of being dominated by a foreign power were not over for Latin America. The United States, Bolívar wrote near the end of his life, seemed "destined by providence to plague America" — he meant Latin America — "with torments in the name of freedom."

2
The Colonies of Iberia

Latin American history goes back almost exactly five hundred years. Christopher Columbus founded the first Spanish colony in the Americas in 1493, on the island of Hispaniola, in what is now the Dominican Republic. The Portuguese colonization of Brazil began after the year 1500.

Spanish and Portuguese holdings in the New World were vast. Brazil alone was, and is, larger than the forty-eight contiguous states from Maine to California. The Spanish colonies extended from Florida on the North American mainland southeastward across the islands of the Caribbean Sea and northward and westward to California's Pacific coast. From there, they swept south through Mexico and tropical Central America and on across the jungles, mountains, and plains of South America to the icy tip of Argentina, only a thousand miles from Antarctica. The Spanish and Portuguese lands were known as the Iberian colonies, because Spain and Portugal are located on Europe's Iberian Peninsula.

For three centuries, Spain and Portugal held their New World colonies. Colonial rule left a deep impression on what we now call Latin America, the countries of the Western Hemisphere that lie south of the United States. Iberian history and Iberian tradition became Latin American history and tradition as well. Understanding both is essential to understanding modern Latin America and its people and problems.

Among the most important of these traditions is that of government by a strong central authority. In sixteenth-, seventeenth-, and eighteenth-century Spain and Portugal, that central authority was an all-powerful monarch.

What is more, the three centuries from 1500 to 1800 were a time when royal supremacy was increasing in the Iberian nations. It was different in some other parts of Europe. In England, for instance, kings and queens were beginning to see a lessening of their royal authority. By the seventeenth century, members of the English Parliament were starting to make their voices heard in matters of laws and taxes. In 1649, radicals in Parliament actually succeeded in deposing a king — Charles I — and having him beheaded.

Such a thing would have been unthinkable in either Spain or Portugal. Spain did have its *cortes*, local organizations that represented members of the clergy, the nobility, and well-to-do city merchants.

The individual *cortes* met separately in various parts of the country, and by the fifteenth century, they were beginning to have some effect on lawmaking, particularly on the setting of taxes. Toward the end of the century, however, they were suppressed by the monarch. Over the next three hundred years, the *cortes* met less frequently, and usually only to offer formal homage to the king. The Portuguese *côrtes* was similarly feeble. For one half-century period, starting in the late 1600s, they did not meet at all. The kings of Portugal reached the high point of their absolute power between 1730 and 1777.

Across the sea, in America, the Spanish and Portuguese monarchs were represented by their viceroys. Each viceroy governed in the name of the king and was responsible only to the king. Serving under each viceroy were military commanders, judges, and other regional and local officials. These officials helped the viceroy with day-to-day administration, but always the viceroy's word was final. This was especially true in the Spanish colonies. There, only the king had the legal right to undo a viceroy's decision, or to remove him from office. In Portuguese Brazil, the situation was somewhat different. In Brazil, the viceroy's word was not absolute, and lesser officials had more authority than in the Spanish colonies.

The royal families of Iberia were conservative in their politics, and in their religion as well. Until the sixteenth century, all of Christian Europe shared one faith, that of the Roman Catholic Church. Then in the early 1500s, the Protestant Reformation began in Germany. By the end of the century, several nations had broken away from Catholicism. Spain and Portugal, however, remained fiercely loyal to the Church. Devotion to Church ritual, and to Church authority, in the Iberian countries grew even stronger in reaction to Protestantism elsewhere. Protestant churches never gained a foothold in Spain or Portugal.

The Spanish and Portuguese brought their conservative Catholicism with them to the New World. Priests and missionaries were diligent in their effort to convert the American "Indians" — so called because the first explorers to reach the New World were convinced they had found India, or "the Indies." Within a few years, the Church was firmly established in the colonies.

The Church did more than spread the Catholic faith in the Americas. It also helped promote authoritarian rule. In the colonies, as back home on the Iberian Peninsula, Church and state were one and the same. Kings and queens believed they ruled by God's divine will. Popes, bishops, and priests believed the same. That made it the Church's duty to uphold royal authority. A devout Christian was a loyal subject of the king. Anyone who disobeyed the king defied God.

It was the same in the Americas. The colonial viceroys were not themselves kings, but since they ruled in the name of the king, they had the full backing of the Church. For more than three hundred years, Roman Catholic Church officials in Latin America stood solidly behind the forces of colonial government.

The Iberian tradition of authoritarian government had far-reaching implications for the colonies. As absolute rulers, the kings of Spain and Portugal insisted upon absolute loyalty from their viceroys and other colonial officers. The only way to be sure of getting such loyalty, they thought, was to appoint men they knew personally to govern in the New World. So colonial rulers were, almost without exception, European rather than American. When one was appointed to a position, he left his home on the Iberian Peninsula, sailed to the New World, and served out his term. Then he returned to his peninsula homeland. As a group, these officials came to be known as *peninsulares* — "peninsulars." In the Americas, the *peninsulares* and their families formed tight little groups that looked down on everyone else, including the *criollos* — the creoles.

The *criollos,* like the *peninsulares,* were of Iberian descent. They, however, had been born in the Americas, the sons and daughters of the soldiers and adventurers who had invaded and conquered the New World. Many *criollos* owned huge tracts of land inherited from ancestors who had received land grants or rewards of gold and silver from monarchs grateful for faithful service. Many were rich and well-educated. Still, they were allowed almost no share in the running of the colonies. That honor was reserved for the European-born *peninsulares.* The highest office generally open to *criollos* was a seat on a *cabildo,* a local town council.

During the 1500s, some *cabildos* showed signs of wanting to assume more power. At once, the Spanish king, who was unwilling to share his royal authority, took away most of their responsibilities. The *cabildos* never recovered, and the *criollos'* only possible path to political power was blocked. They were cut off from government and denied the opportunity to rule themselves.

In this, the Latin experience was very different from that of the English colonies in North America. Almost from the outset, settlers in the northern colonies were able to experiment with self-government. As time passed, they won the right to choose their own representatives to colonial assemblies or legislatures. Political issues were discussed and argued about in public. From the discussions came separate and distinct political ideas and philosophies. Out of the philosophies, political groups began to grow. These groups were the forerunners of our modern political parties.

In the authoritarian Iberian colonies, political debate was not encouraged. During much of the colonial period, censorship kept people from reading or hearing things their rulers did not want them to read or hear. In each viceroyalty, only one way of thinking was encouarged. That was the king's way. There was just one political party — the king's. No organized opposition party could establish itself.

Yet opposition to colonial rule did exist in the Spanish and Portuguese colonies. It came in a form that many of us today think of as typically Latin American: sparked by a strong, charismatic leader, centered around a single issue, and generally violent. This kind of opposition grew naturally out of the political conditions under which the people of the region were forced to live.

Since the Iberian nations and their colonies had no representative legislatures, colonial laws were drawn up by a Royal and Supreme Council of Indies. The Spanish council was established in 1524; the Portuguese, in 1604. The Spanish council was especially busy. During its first hundred years, it wrote almost five hundred thousand laws. These covered every aspect of colonial life, from taxes to Church affairs, from economics to the military, from bookkeeping procedures to official appointments.

Any organization that creates an average of nearly five thousand laws a year is sure to come up with a number that are unfair or unwise — or simply unenforceable. This is particularly true if the lawmakers live three thousand miles away from the land for which they are setting down the rules. Over and over the Council of Indies published laws that the *criollos* found oppressive and unacceptable.

When that happened, the *criollos* reacted quickly and violently. Revolts were not uncommon in the American colonies. Some uprisings were directed against new laws or taxes, while others were aimed at the *peninsulares* who tried to enforce the laws or collect the taxes. But every time, the unrest had one narrow, specific goal: Abolish that tax. Remove that official. Change that law.

Frequently, the revolts worked. The tax was lifted; the official recalled; the law altered. And so the pattern became set. To many in Latin America, revolution came to be an almost normal part of everyday politics. In a way, it took the place of representative government. Instead of working to change conditions through an elected legislature, *criollos* took their complaints to the streets in riot and revolution.

This is very different from using revolution as a means of bringing about wide social reform or to change an entire political system. In the United States, for example, the revolution of 1776 freed the colonies from the English crown and allowed them to become a democracy. The Russian Revolution of 1917 ended in the overthrow of the czar and turned Russia into a communist state. But in Latin America, revolution usually had a more limited purpose.

There, it tended to take the place of political debate and party action as part of the routine political process.

With revolts and uprisings so much a part of ordinary politics, violence became a part of it as well. Not that Latin Americans are an especially violent people. Over the years, the nations of Europe have experienced more wars, and bigger wars, than the Latin countries have. But a visitor to a Latin American city has usually been likelier to hear about violence in the streets, or to witness a political demonstration that turns into a bloody riot, than has a tourist in London, Amsterdam, or Stockholm.

Along with violence in political life came militarism — the tendency of governments to rely upon military might to maintain their authority. Ever suspecting unrest, and ever fearful of it, peninsular authorities and administrators often called upon their troops to keep the peace. The Latin tradition of a strong military, like its traditions of political violence and a powerful and repressive central authority, has roots that go back to the very beginnings of Spanish and Portuguese rule in the New World.

Other aspects of the Iberian legacy have less to do with institutions than with individuals. They have evolved from the kind of people who set sail for the Spanish and Portuguese colonies and with their reasons for doing so.

Why do people tear up their roots to settle in a

strange new world far away? For many of the early colonists in what is now the United States, the answer was: to find a place where we can worship God as we please. The Pilgrims and Puritans of Massachusetts, the Baptists of Rhode Island, the Catholics of Maryland, all came to North America in search of religious freedom. For the Iberian settlers to the south, the answer was different. "People did not come to [Latin America] to be free, as they had to the United States," says a twentieth-century scientist and university professor who lives in Argentina. The professor, who opposes some of the policies of his government, spoke anonymously to a representative of the Federation of American Scientists. "They were, as Catholics in the Catholic countries from which they came, already free from persecution. Instead they came to get rich."

Not only did many of the early Spanish and Portuguese *conquistadores* — conquerors — come to the New World to get rich, they came to get rich quick. In his classic *History of the Conquest of Mexico,* the nineteenth-century historian William H. Prescott relates a story about Hernando Cortez, the man who won Mexico for the Spanish king. Cortez led the Spanish soldiers who defeated the Aztecs — the Indians who had earlier conquered Mexico and who ruled it as a great empire. After his final victory over the Aztecs in 1521, the *conquistador* applied to Mexico's peninsular authorities for a reward. The governor's secretary assured Cortez that he would receive a generous grant of land. Cortez was incensed. "But I came to get gold," he fumed, "not to till the soil, like a peasant."

Most *conquistadores* shared Cortez's attitude. They were adventurers and professional soldiers who disdained physical labor. Some were the illegitimate sons of noble families. Others, though of low birth, pretended to be of noble stock. Being illegitimate, or from poor families, they had no hope of inheriting wealth or position. Being noble, or wishing to appear so, they refused to dirty their hands working for a living. In the Old World, these idle, boastful men were treated insultingly and with contempt.

But in the New World, they were proud and mighty warriors. Mounted on horseback, encased in glittering armor, they could terrify the Indians they came upon — or trick them into believing they were gods. They could seize the Indians' treasure by force — or obtain it by guile. With luck, they could make a fortune overnight.

Many of the king's peninsular officers also saw the New World as a place in which to become rich. Selling lesser offices to ambitious *conquistadores* and accepting bribes were two of the most common ways to make money. Even Church missionaries, while not necessarily hoping to become rich themselves, might seek to glorify God by converting American gold and silver into religious ornaments and statues. And above all, there were the kings and queens back home, the monarchs who expected their colonies to be profitable. For three hundred years, those monarchs made sure to keep a steady procession of treasure-filled galleons eastward-bound across the Atlantic Ocean.

Of course, not all those involved with the colonies had purely selfish motives. There were *conquistadores* who wanted to serve king and country, *peninsulares* who tried to rule wisely, churchmen who wished only to Christianize the Indians. Yet alongside the good intentions there was almost always the desire to find treasure, to make a fortune, to grow rich without working, to provide adornment for God's cathedrals. This desire led to the molding of the kind of society that still exists in Latin America.

The Spanish and Portuguese wish for wealth guaranteed that the Aztecs and others they found living in the Americas would first be conquered and then treated harshly. Never mind that some Indian civilizations were among the greatest the world has known. Never mind that the Aztecs developed a number system that was, in some ways, more flexible than our own. Never mind that the Incas of mountainous Peru designed and built monuments so massive and in such hard-to-reach spots that no one today can figure out how they did it. Never mind the great stone calendars, the elaborate irrigation ditches, the fertile farms, the systems of welfare, the intricate and beautiful art. All that was nothing compared to the Europeans' belief that the Aztecs and the Incas possessed vast stores of gold and silver.

In pursuit of that gold and silver, the *conquistadores* ambushed and massacred. They tore down palaces and holy places. They smashed works of art and melted them down. They persuaded friendly Indian rulers to reveal their secret riches, then seized those riches and betrayed the owners' friendship. All the while, the treasure flowed into their pockets and across the sea to fill the royal coffers.

But in an amazingly short time, the Indians' treasure — never as great as the *conquistadores* believed it to be — ran out. Now, in order to keep the riches coming, it was necessary to sink great mine shafts into the hills and mountains of the Americas.

Mining is dirty and dangerous work, and the *conquistadores* never considered doing it themselves. Why should they, when the Indians could do it for them? In only a few years, the original inhabitants of Mexico and of Central and South America were no longer the masters of great civilizations. They had sunk into a condition that was almost slavery.

That it was not quite slavery was thanks to the Catholic Church. The Church saw its New World mission as that of saving Indian souls by bringing them to Christ, and its officers convinced the king that it was impossible to convert people and enslave them at the same time. So instead of slavery, the

Spanish adopted a system of labor called the *encomienda.*

In theory, the *encomienda* protected the Indians. Under it, numbers of them were entrusted to various *conquistadores* or officials. The Europeans were expected to see to it that the Indians received religious instruction and were fed and clothed. In return, the Indians would work for their "protectors."

Such an arrangement was sure to be abused. Overworked, poorly fed and cared for, and subject to terrible outbreaks of diseases brought from Europe by the *conquistadores,* thousands of Indians soon died. Those who did not frequently rose up in rebellion. The revolts were put down with ferocious cruelty. In everything but name, the Indians were slaves.

Slavery also existed under its own name in the colonies. The Church did not prevent the buying and selling of black men and women, and thousands of Africans were captured and transported to the New World. Most were forced to work in the seacoast areas of Central and South America and on the Caribbean islands, where the climates were most like those of their native lands. Slavery was legal throughout the colonial period in Latin America (as it was in the English colonies of North America). Abolished in most of the region during the 1820s (well before it was outlawed in the United States), it remained in force in Brazil until 1889. The *enco-*

mienda had ended earlier, during the first part of the eighteenth century.

Even without the *encomienda,* however, the Indians had no real freedom. Strict laws kept them from moving about as they pleased. They still owed a certain amount of labor to the white man. Besides that, informal systems, such as debt peonage, served to maintain their low status.

Under debt peonage, a wealthy man would offer a poor one a plot of land and a job. The plot would be tiny and the pay low, but the employer would give those who worked for him generous credit to buy food and whatever else they needed to live. As soon as a worker ran up a debt, he was stuck, unable to leave his job until the money was repaid. Only rarely did anyone manage to break free of debt peonage. The wealthy man's labor force remained intact.

So did his wealth and position. While the vast majority of blacks, Indians, and *mestizos* — people of mixed European and Indian blood — were trapped in servitude and poverty, a very small number of *criollos* became just as firmly entrenched at the top of the economic ladder. These few wealthy people owned huge *haciendas* — estates — which their slaves or Indians who were subject to the *encomienda* (and later their debt-ridden tenants) farmed or ranched for them. Some also owned mines, banks, and other profitable businesses.

This kind of society — one in which most land

and wealth is owned by a few and the majority of people are bound to the landed wealthy and compelled to serve them in return for a bare living — is called feudal. During the Middle Ages, which lasted from the fifth century A.D. to about the middle of the fifteenth century, most of Europe was organized along feudal lines. The lord in his castle owned much property. His serfs, who owned neither the land they worked nor the homes they lived in, labored for him. The lord might become richer or he might grow poorer, but the serfs' condition never changed. For a thousand years, laws all over Europe protected feudal ways.

By the 1500s, though, things were changing in much of Europe. Trade became more important and cities grew. Scientific discoveries were made. Industry developed. In some places, kings began to see a lessening of their power and there was movement toward self-government. Feudalism was dying out.

Not in Spain and Portugal, however. The Iberian kings and queens were becoming stronger and squelching any democratic tendencies within their lands. The rulers' conservatism and the teachings of the Catholic Church helped keep out scientific and trade. Feudal laws continued to be enforced by the state and upheld by the Church.

Not only did Iberian feudalism outlast feudalism in many other parts of Europe, but the Iberian nations were also able to transfer much of the system to their American colonies. During three centuries of colonial rule, feudalism continued to be the way of life in Latin America. Only in a few places did the Iberian legacy become mixed with other influences. Some parts of Central America and northeastern South America were eventually colonized by England, France, and Holland. So were some islands of the Caribbean Sea. Elsewhere throughout Latin America, however, Iberian values and traditions remained undisturbed.

Nevertheless, changes were in store for the area. In 1783, one of the men destined to help bring those changes about was born in Caracas, in the colony of Venezuela. His name was Simón Bolívar. By coincidence, Bolívar, who was to play a leading role in liberating Latin America from Spain, was born in the very year the United States officially won its independence from England.

Bolívar grew up in the feudal colonial society created by three centuries of Iberian rule. His was a *criollo* family, aristocratic and wealthy. Yet as *criollos,* the Bolívars and others like them had little political power or influence in their own land. Government, after three hundred years of colonialism, was still in the hands of the *peninsulares.*

Slowly, *criollo* resentment grew. During Bolívar's boyhood, that resentment was fanned by news of the American Revolution and of the democratic constitution adopted by the new United States. A few radical *criollos* began to talk of the possibility of independence for the Iberian colonies, as well. Still, in the early 1800s, only a few of them had any serious wish to break away from their mother countries.

Events in Europe soon changed that. In 1804, Napoleon Bonaparte became emperor of France. Napoleon, a politician and soldier, dreamed of conquering all Europe. In 1807, his armies invaded Portugal. The Portuguese royal family packed up and fled to Brazil. In a way, that was the moment Brazil won its freedom, for although the king eventually returned to his home, his son never did. In 1822, that son became Pedro I, emperor of Brazil. The country was independent from then on.

For the Spanish colonies, matters were more confused. In 1808, Napoleon imprisoned the Spanish king and his son, the crown prince. He placed his own brother, Joseph Bonaparte, on the Spanish throne. A revolution broke out.

But it broke out in Spain, not in the New World. All over Spain, angry people rose up against the Bonapartes. Local committees — *juntas* — were organized to provide leadership for the rebels. By late 1813, these rebels had pretty well driven the French out of the country, and less than two years later, Napoleon met his final defeat at Waterloo. The Spanish crown prince, released from jail in 1814, ruled the country as Fernando VII until 1833.

Meantime, what about Spain's colonies? At first,

even with their rightful king in captivity, Spanish officers there had managed to keep the viceroyalties running almost as if nothing had happened. By 1810, though, the situation was deteriorating. If the *criollos* had resented the *peninsulares* when they ruled in the name of the king, they resented them even more now that they were ruling on behalf of the *juntas. Criollo* revolts broke out in some of the larger colonial cities. In 1811, Venezuela became the first Spanish-American colony to declare itself free. Simón Bolívar — *El Libertador* — was a leader in that independence movement and in others that followed.

But liberty did not come quickly for the Spanish colonies. By 1814, a lawful king again sat on the Spanish throne. And Fernando VII was determined to crush the spreading rebellion.

If Spain had not been so badly weakened, first by Napoleon's invasion and then by the fighting against him, Fernando might have succeeded. As it was, he could not transport enough loyal troops to the New World to do the job. Because of this, the colonies' wars of independence were fought largely between those *criollos* who were sick of peninsular rule and peninsular arrogance, and the king's officers who sought to maintain their authority. In a way, they were more like civil wars than revolutions.

The last crucial battle for independence came on December 9, 1824, at Ayacucho, in a valley deep in the Andes Mountains of Peru. The *criollos* won at

Ayacucho, and the Spanish colonies — except for such Caribbean islands as Cuba and Puerto Rico — were free.

And already, the young United States was pledging itself to see that they stayed that way.

3

The United States
and Latin America:
The View from the North

Even before the battle of Ayacucho — even before
Venezuela's declaration of independence in 1811 —
the United States had put itself firmly behind the
idea of freedom for the Spanish colonies. Back in
1808, President Thomas Jefferson had ordered U.S.
representatives in Mexico to let it be known, unofficially, that this country would adopt a friendly attitude toward any independence movement there. In
1822, the United States became the first nation in the
world to recognize an independent Mexico. The
United States was equally supportive of liberation
movements in other parts of Spanish America, and
by 1826, it had recognized just about all its nations
as independent.

It had done more. On December 2, 1823, President
James Monroe had sent a message to Congress. The
message included two passages that, together, came
to be known as the Monroe Doctrine.

No longer, the president said, would the imperialistic — empire-building — nations of Europe be free

to establish colonies in the New World. If any tried, the United States would step in and stop them. The Monroe Doctrine was a warning to the world that the United States intended to protect the freedom of the Americas. From now on, European countries had better stay out of Western Hemisphere affairs.

In 1823, there seemed to be good reason to issue that warning. Spain's King Fernando VII was still struggling to regain his colonies. Rulers of other nations, too, seemed prepared to try to grab some of Spain's old empire for themselves. In 1815, several of these rulers had joined together in what they called the Holy Alliance. An attempt by that alliance to seize and rule part of North or South America would pose a threat to the United States, Monroe thought. "It is impossible," he told Congress, "that the allied powers should extend their political system to any portion of either continent without endangering our peace and happiness."

Why might such an extension of foreign rule harm the United States? Because, Monroe answered, no one can "believe that our southern brethren, if left to themselves, would adopt it of their own accord." In other words, the United States must help the new republics maintain their independence, because those republics would surely never surrender it without a fight. And such a fight could jeopardize the United States. However, the president also made it clear that this country had no intention of trying to overturn European rule where it already existed in the New World. Spain was perfectly free to maintain its Cuban and Puerto Rican colonies, for instance. Denmark would still govern the Virgin Islands, as it had since 1672. England, France, and Holland could keep their small colonial holdings as well. Even today, the United States backs some European claims in Latin America. In 1982, this country sided with England against Argentina in a dispute over the Falkland Islands, three hundred miles east of Argentina. Both countries claimed the islands, which the Argentines call the Malvinas. After a short war, the Falklands remained in British hands.

Over the years, the Monroe Doctrine has been invoked many times. In 1824, the United States attacked a pirate stronghold in Puerto Rico. Nine years later, U.S. troops were landed in Argentina during an uprising there, and three years after that, they went ashore in Peru.

Not only did the United States find it necessary to act frequently under the Monroe Doctrine, it found it needed to expand upon the doctrine from time to time. One expansion came about when Texas broke away from Mexico.

Texas was Mexican until 1835. In that year, the territory rebelled, and in 1836, Texans declared themselves independent. But the Lone Star Republic did not enjoy a long life. From the first, many Texans, and many in this country, too, wanted to see Texas become part of the United States.

Europeans, on the other hand, were not enthusiastic about the idea. France and England were particularly anxious for Texas to remain independent. As a separate republic, they thought, Texas would act as a counterbalance to the fast-growing United States. "We need independent states, a balance of power," the French prime minister declared.

Not so, the United States responded. On December 2, 1843, twenty years to the day after President Monroe had issued his famous statement, President James K. Polk sent a message of his own to Congress. In it, he spoke of the French call for a balance of power. Such a balance "cannot be permitted to have any application on the North American continent," he stated. France and England had no business interfering — even with words — between Texas and the United States. Two years later, Texas was admitted to the Union.

In its expanded form, the Monroe Doctrine continued to be applied to Latin American affairs. During the second half of the nineteenth century, the United States intervened militarily in Latin America nearly fifty times. Then, in 1904, another U.S. president enlarged the scope of the doctrine once again.

The president was Theodore Roosevelt, and his

action came about as the result of a problem in Venezuela. In 1902, the government of that country was accused by England and Germany of failing to repay money it had borrowed from them. In an effort to collect the debt, England and Germany sent ships to block Venezuelan harbors.

This affront to the Monroe Doctrine angered many in the United States. President Roosevelt shared the outrage, and on December 6, 1904, he issued what came to be known as the Roosevelt corollary to the Monroe Doctrine. In it, he admitted that "chronic wrongdoing" — such as the nonpayment of a debt — might well "require intervention by some civilized nation." However, in the Western Hemisphere, that "civilized nation" could only be the United States. No European power could be permitted to act against any American republic for any reason. Therefore, Roosevelt concluded, if the United States ever had reason to believe that an action by a Latin American country might provoke a future European intervention, it would have to move in ahead of time to correct whatever the problem was.

The Roosevelt corollary got a quick workout. In 1905, the Dominican Republic was deeply in debt to various European countries. Fearing this might lead to unwelcome intervention, the United States offered to take over Dominican finances temporarily and straighten them out. Two United States warships anchored off the nation's capital city helped persuade Dominican leaders to agree to the plan.

In the years since then, the United States has continued to put the Monroe Doctrine to use. Throughout the twentieth century and particularly during the second half of the century, the doctrine has been used to rid the hemisphere of left-wing political movements. U.S. troops put down a leftist uprising in Nicaragua in 1909, for example. In 1926, they put down another, this one led by a Nicaraguan rebel named Augusto César Sandino. On occasion, this country's armed forces have been dispatched to Mexico, Haiti, Cuba, Panama, Honduras, and other countries. In 1954, U.S. troops were called upon to quell what President Dwight Eisenhower saw as the threat of a communist takeover in Guatemala.

Important as the Monroe Doctrine has been to the U.S. effort to keep the peace in Latin America, it has not been this country's only instrument of policy in the region. Trade has been important, too.

In the beginning, establishing U.S.–Latin American trading relations was not easy. When Latin America won its independence, most of its trade was with England. Slowly, that changed. The United States and its industries grew rapidly during the nineteenth century. U.S. factories produced more and more manufactured goods. They required more and more raw materials. U.S. industrialists needed to buy and import more of the latter, and to export and sell more of the former. Where better to do both than right in their own back yard — in Latin America? One nineteenth-century U.S. secretary of state, James G. Blaine, summed up business's attitude succinctly: "It is the especial province of this country to improve and expand its trade with the nations of America."

Improve and expand its Latin trade is exactly what the United States did. Companies poured money into developing the area's natural resources: oil in Mexico, Venezuela, and Bolivia; tin in Bolivia; copper in Chile. Food and agricultural products were important, too. Cotton was grown in Mexico and Peru, and sugar in Cuba. In 1899, the United Fruit Company of Boston began investing in large banana-growing plantations in Central America and tropical South America. United Fruit was a business giant, running its own private railroad lines and owning large port facilities, as well as farmland. So huge were United Fruit operations in some Central and South American nations that those nations came to be known, in the United States, as "banana republics."

Trade between the United States and Latin America continued to prosper in this century. "By the 1930s," says one economic historian from this country, "the bulk of the productive mineral resources" of Latin America were owned by U.S. companies. In 1929, U.S. businesses had $5.5 billion invested in Latin America. Thirty years later, that figure had reached more than $9 billion.

A number of Latin Americans have warmly welcomed these investments in their countries. U.S. capital — money — has built mines and turned trackless jungle into productive farmland. It has provided markets for the area's rich natural resources. It has brought modern technology and expertise into nations that have needed both. It has meant jobs for thousands of men and women. In general, the leaders of the Latin republics have shown themselves willing to do all they could to attract U.S. investors and to keep them happy.

U.S. politicians, too, have encouraged investment in Latin America. The monetary benefits of such a policy are obvious. But there are other advantages as well. The more U.S. companies invest in Latin America, the less room there is for European business to expand there. Less European investment in the region means less chance of European political intervention. Thus, the United States policy of favoring investment in Latin America works to reinforce the Monroe Doctrine.

By the early twentieth century, this investment-encouraging policy had come to be known as "dollar diplomacy." Its usefulness to United States interests was described by one newspaperman in 1911:

"When an American republic is on the brink of bankruptcy, no friendlier or politically wiser action could be taken by the United States than to seek, through . . . American capital, by one stroke to remove all question of European intervention, and at the same time to start the country concerned upon the road to progress, peace, and prosperity."

Yet in spite of the benefits of dollar diplomacy and the protection offered by the Monroe Doctrine, Latin America has not been entirely free of unfriendly attentions from Europe. As we saw, Cuba and Puerto Rico were still Spanish colonies when the doctrine was proclaimed in 1823. At that time, President Monroe made it clear that the United States had no intention of interfering with Spanish rule there. By the end of the nineteenth century, however, the situation had altered.

In 1868, the Cuban people rebelled against their European masters. After a bloody ten-year war, the revolt was put down. It was renewed in 1895, and again suppressed. Spanish forces under the command of General Valeriano Weyler began a cruel campaign aimed at stamping out the rebellion once and for all.

Newspapers in the United States carried vivid, detailed — and frequently exaggerated — reports of Weyler's brutality, reports that aroused strong anti-Spanish feelings in this country. Then, in February

1898, the U.S. battleship *Maine* was blown up in the harbor at Havana, capital of Cuba. Two hundred sixty sailors were killed.

Were the Spanish responsible? Most in the United States were convinced they were, and "Remember the *Maine!*" became a call to arms. On April 20, Congress resolved that if the Spanish would not agree to pull out of Cuba of their own accord, they must be driven out. The Spanish did not agree, and the Spanish-American War began.

It was over quickly, in just three months. Among the United States war heroes was Colonel Theodore Roosevelt, soon to be President Theodore Roosevelt. It was Colonel Roosevelt who led the Rough Riders in their victorious charge up San Juan Hill in eastern Cuba. By July, Spain had given up the fight and Cuba and Puerto Rico were no longer Spanish colonies.

It was not long before further European interest in American affairs led the United States to help another Latin country gain independence. In this case, the European powers were England and France, and what they were interested in was building a canal across the Central American isthmus. Until then, ships traveling between the east and west coasts of the Americas had to sail all the way around the South American continent and fight their way through the narrow and dangerous Strait of Magellan. The voyage took weeks, and many ships were lost during the stormy passage.

The idea of building a cross-isthmus waterway had been around for many years, and a French company had even started work on a canal in 1881. However, poor planning and devastating illness among the workers had forced the French to cancel the project. Now, as the twentieth century began, the United States determined to revive the idea. This country was fast turning into a world power, and a world power must be able to move its ships, both freighters and warships, quickly and efficiently around the globe. A canal was imperative.

And it was imperative that that canal be built by — and owned and controlled by — the United States itself. If the French or English controlled it, they might one day decide to close it and deny passage to United States vessels. What a violation of the Monroe Doctrine that would be! In 1901, England agreed to a treaty that gave the United States the sole right to build and fortify a canal. Soon afterward, the United States convinced France to sell out her canal rights, as well.

Now all that remained was for the United States to work out an agreement with Colombia, upon whose soil the canal would be situated. President Roosevelt offered to purchase a "canal zone" in the Colombian territory of Panama. In addition, the president promised that the United States would pay an annual "rent" in return for the right to occupy that zone.

The Colombian Senate turned Roosevelt's offer down, claiming that it was not generous enough. This rejection disappointed some in Panama, and, encouraged by the U.S. government, they rose up in revolt against the Colombian government. The date was November 3, 1903.

Seventy-two hours later, it was all over. Panama was independent. The United States recognized the new nation that very day and work on the canal soon began. It was completed in 1914.

Another aspect to U.S. dealings with Latin America has been this country's effort to promote a spirit of Pan-Americanism. *Pan* is the ancient Greek word for "all," and Pan-Americanism aims to provide ways for all the nations of America to cooperate and to work together as allies. The first U.S.-sponsored Pan-American conference took place in 1889.

Others soon followed. Over the years, North, South, and Central American delegates to the conferences have hammered out various agreements, particularly agreements having to do with international trade. But there has been more to Pan-Americanism than that.

Perhaps the most successful promoter of Pan-Americanism was President Franklin D. Roosevelt. In his first inaugural address, delivered in 1933,

Roosevelt spoke of his desire to build an inter-American system "of which confidence, friendship, and good will are the cornerstones." Pan-Americanism, he declared, meant being a "good neighbor."

President Roosevelt followed a Good Neighbor policy throughout his twelve years in office. During that time, the United States drastically reduced the number of its armed interventions that had begun under the Monroe Doctrine. In 1933, Roosevelt withdrew the troops that had been sent to Nicaragua in 1926. The United States also agreed to give up certain privileges it had enjoyed in Cuba, Panama, and other nations. Finally, the U.S. government offered the nations of Latin America help in developing their economies; in improving transportation, education, and public health; and in entering the technological world of the mid-twentieth century. These activities were carried out by the coordinator of the Office of Inter-American Affairs. During the early 1940s this position was occupied by Nelson A. Rockefeller, whose family had long had multimillion-dollar business holdings in Latin America.

When World War II broke out in 1939, Roosevelt put more emphasis than ever before upon Pan-Americanism, and upon cultivating unity among the nations of the Western Hemisphere. He urged the Latin countries to stand firm against the threat from the enemy Axis powers — Germany, Italy, and Japan. Eventually, the president had his way. By the time the war ended in 1945, all the nations of America had agreed to back the United States and its allies.

With the war over, the United States continued to press for Pan-American cooperation. The United Nations was established in 1945, and within it, the Organization of American States (OAS). Membership in the OAS is limited to the nations of this hemisphere. The group's purpose is to promote American well-being. Its charter also provides for mutual defense among all member nations. If one is attacked or threatened by an outside force, it may call upon the other OAS countries for help.

Additional U.S.–Latin American treaty agreements reinforce the OAS and the idea of mutual defense. They protect the area, not just against armed attack, but also against "aggression which is not armed attack." Such aggression might be an attempt by a political group — a communist organization, for example — to take over a nation's government by questionable or illegal means. Still other postwar Pan-American agreements deal with trade.

Inter-American agreements continue to be worked out today. In August 1983, for instance, President Ronald Reagan signed the Caribbean Basin Initiative, an arrangement under which the United States promised to provide economic aid and favorable trade deals to twenty-seven Latin countries, many of them small Caribbean nations. Subjects for future

Pan-American treaties might include the international drug trade and the problem of illegal immigration into the United States.

Both drugs and immigration have been increasingly troublesome in the 1970s and 1980s. Much of the marijuana and cocaine sold and used in this country comes from South and Central America. U.S. officials have been frustrated by the failure of Latin American governments to take steps to halt the flow. As for illegal immigrants, thousands of them try to enter the United States each year, most of them by way of Mexico. The immigrants come to this country looking for work. Jobs with decent wages are scarce in Latin America. But U.S. workers complain that every illegal alien who finds employment here takes a job away from a U.S. citizen.

Illegal immigration and illicit drugs are sore points between the United States and the Latin countries. Still, these problems are only a small part of the picture of overall Western Hemisphere relations. From the point of view of the United States, those relations have generally been good. From the beginning, the United States promoted freedom in Latin America. It has protected the area's independent republics from European conquest and from domination by communism. It has encouraged prosperity-building investment and fostered a spirit of friendship and cooperation within the hemisphere. The past two hundred years, most people in the United States feel, have provided the basis for future cordial relations between this country and its southern neighbors.

Not all Latin Americans would agree with this picture of U.S.-Latin relations, however. Neither would a number of people in this country. In their view, the United States' interest in their part of the world amounts to simple self-interest. From the start, they say, the United States has regarded Latin America as an area whose resources are to be exploited, whose problems can be ignored, and whose people may be treated with scorn.

4

The United States and Latin America: The View from the South

Why should Latin Americans think of themselves as having been scorned, ignored, and exploited by the United States? Most people in this country regard themselves as the best friends and protectors Latin America has. But consider the history of relations between the United States and Latin America from the Latin perspective.

During most of the time the New World was being colonized, England and Spain were rivals. Both had strong navies, and each was determined to see its fleet rule the waves. Throughout much of the seventeenth century, English adventurers like Sir Francis Drake and Sir Henry Morgan harassed the Spanish galleons sailing the Atlantic, often capturing rich treasures of gold and silver. In the Americas, the two countries squabbled over territorial rights. Florida, for instance, belonged first to Spain, then to England, then, after 1783, to Spain again.

When the United States won its independence, it looked as if the old rivalries would continue between the Iberian colonies and this new English-speaking country. Latin Americans had other concerns, as well. One involved the obvious intention of the United States to expand its territory. It seemed likely to Latin Americans that this expansion would take place at their expense. It did, starting in 1803.

That was the year in which President Thomas Jefferson purchased the Louisiana Territory from Napoleon. This country agreed to pay the French emperor $15 million. In return, it got a piece of land that stretched from New Orleans to the Rocky Mountains. The territory covered nearly 830,000 square miles.

Louisiana was Napoleon's to sell because he had, three years earlier, forced Spain to give it to France. For nearly forty years before that, the territory had belonged to Spain. Naturally, Spain, and Mexico, which bordered on Louisiana, were dismayed by the purchase. Overnight, the United States had doubled in size. Spanish interests, and Spanish pride, had suffered a blow.

They suffered another one sixteen years later, when the United States took over Spanish Florida. Again, the United States paid for the land. Spain got $5 million. But the sale took place only after Spain had decided it could no longer defend its territory from repeated U.S. Army raids.

So perhaps the *criollos* did not look at U.S. support for their independence movements in exactly the way United States citizens themselves did. Perhaps they suspected that this country was eager to get Spain and Portugal out of the Americas simply in order to add to its own possessions. Perhaps they didn't see the Monroe Doctrine as the United States saw it, either. Maybe they thought it signaled a U.S. resolve to make itself supreme in the hemisphere.

If so, their suspicions must have been strengthened when President Polk announced his extension of the Monroe Doctrine and the United States snapped up Texas. The following year, 1846, Polk ordered troops into an area just north of the Rio Grande, the river that today separates Mexico from Texas. Mexico claimed this territory as its own, and sent a force to defend it. The U.S. soldiers defeated the Mexicans and forced them to retreat south across the river. Then the U.S. force chased after them, entering what was, beyond any doubt, Mexican territory.

To Polk, this series of events added up to a Mexican invasion of the United States. Mexicans had "shed American blood on American soil," he told Congress. Agreeing, Congress resolved that, "by the act of the republic of Mexico a state of war exists."

The Mexican-American War lasted eighteen months and ended with the United States annexing California and most of New Mexico. Mexicans were angered by the loss of territory. Besides that, they were insulted by the U.S. claim that *they* had started the war. Even in the United States, some sympathized with their sense of outrage. Abraham Lincoln, then a member of Congress, called Polk's charge that Mexico had done the invading "sheerest nonsense."

In 1853, the United States completed its taking of Mexican land with an agreement called the Gadsden Purchase. Under it, this country bought what are now the southern parts of Arizona and New Mexico for $10 million. All told, by 1853, the United States had acquired over half of what had once been Mexico.

Nor was the outright buying or seizing of territory the only matter that bothered the people of the southern republics. Many were deeply disturbed by U.S.–Latin American trade relations and by the direction those relations were taking.

From the start, the United States was a richer, more highly industrialized nation than any in Latin America. It had many factories. U.S. industrialists owned the most up-to-date machinery. They knew how to take advantage of new technologies as they came along, and how to adapt those technologies to their needs. Latin America, on the other hand, had just two things to offer. The area had plenty of natural resources. And it had plenty of people so poor that they were willing to work in the mines and on the plantations for very, very little pay. Latin America's feudal legacy of slavery, the *encomienda,* and debt peonage made it easy for U.S. capitalists to step in and pick up where the Iberian kings and their peninsular officers had left off.

Of course, the capitalists had something to offer Latin America, too. They did put a great deal of money into the area. They did develop its mines, its farms, its timber, its oil fields. They did offer jobs to thousands.

But the development benefited the United States more than it did Latin Americans. It was United States citizens who owned the mines, the plantations, the forestlands. The tin, the copper, the oil, all left Latin America and made their way to the United States and other countries. So did the lumber, the bananas, and the sugar. Latins were left with only their poor wages.

One person who has made a study of inter-American trade relations is Carlos Fuentes, a Mexican writer and diplomat. According to Fuentes, in a typical mid-twentieth-century year, United States business might make a $775 million profit in Latin America. Of that, $575 million would go back to the north. Only $200 million would stay in the south. In one seven-year period alone, Fuentes calculates, Latin America lost close to $3 billion to the United States that way. In Latin eyes, U.S.–Latin American trade is a one-way street. "Where is the real benefit for our economies?" Fuentes demands.

Yet if the bargain is so bad for Latin America, why did governments there allow it? Why did they encourage so much foreign investment? Because they certainly did encourage it. During the nineteenth and early twentieth centuries, the leaders of many Latin nations rewrote their tax laws to spare U.S. firms and save them money. They exempted U.S. businesspeople from other laws, as well, permitting them to write, and do, and say, things that were forbidden to their own people. They ignored the needs of their citizens, allowing them, for instance, to work for U.S. companies at starvation wages. When the workers tried to form unions and demand higher pay, their own governments sent the army and police to stop them, often with violence. Why would any nation's leaders act this way?

The answer is simple, angry Latin Americans respond. Latin leaders cooperated with U.S. business because they knew that the U.S. government wanted them to. And because they knew that if they did not cooperate, they would not remain in power very long.

Latin Americans see a pattern in this. Over the years, U.S. government and business have worked together to get people who were friendly to the United States into office in Latin America. Then they did anything that might be necessary to keep them there, including using armed force. Of course, this pattern did not spring into being full-blown. It came into existence gradually, starting in the early years of the Latin republics.

Independence in Latin America, unlike independence in the United States, did not mean a movement toward a democratic form of government. During their first hundred years of independence, a majority of Latin American nations suffered under a succession of brutal dictators. There were exceptions: Chile had a just and stable government through most of the nineteenth century, and Brazil was a constitutional monarchy until 1889. But for most of the region, the nineteenth century was the age of the *caudillo* — the strongman. The Spanish word *caudillo* refers to the leader of an armed band.

The *caudillos* were rough, crude men, interested mainly in winning power, wealth, and glory for themselves. Their people's welfare was of little concern to them. As long as they could stay in office, stashing away large sums of money in private bank accounts, they were content. In many ways, the *caudillos* were like the *conquistadores* of old. They resembled some of the *peninsulares,* too, with their eagerness to use public office as a path to wealth.

One way they found to enrich themselves was to sell business rights to U.S. interests. It was the Mexican *caudillo* Antonio López de Santa Anna, for instance, who agreed to the Gadsden Purchase of 1853. U.S. railroad tycoons wanted to construct a line to the Pacific across Mexican land. Santa Anna wanted money. The deal was struck. Other deals in other countries permitted U.S. business to control more and more Latin American land and resources. Remember the estimate of one historian that by the 1930s, "the bulk" of Latin America's mineral resources belonged to United States citizens.

Sometimes, that ownership was threatened. A friendly dictator might be overthrown and his place taken by someone with an interest in trying to improve his people's standard of living. Such a person might announce his intention of taking over U.S. businesses and running them for the benefit of Latin Americans. Or the new leader might want to divert the profits into his own pocket. Or there might not even be a new leader at all, just the possibility that one might try to seize power. But whatever the precise situation, the threat might arise. U.S. business interests might appear to be under attack.

Fortunately for the owners of those businesses, the consequences of such an attack could be avoided. The owners would complain to the U.S. government that their holdings were in danger. The response would be automatic. A threat to U.S. property in Latin America amounted to a threat to the United States itself. A threat to the United States meant the Monroe Doctrine must be invoked. Send in the Marines!

And the Marines were sent in, time and again. Take the decade of the 1850s. In 1852 and 1853, they landed in Argentina. In 1853, 1854, and 1857, they were sent to Nicaragua. In 1855, it was Uruguay.

And it was Uruguay again three years later. In 1856, the Marines were put ashore in Panama, and in 1859, in Paraguay and Mexico. "Gunboat diplomacy" is the name that has been given to the almost constant use of U.S. troops to protect U.S. interests in Latin America during the nineteenth century.

The United States continued to rely upon gunboat diplomacy as the nineteenth-century *caudillos* gave way to twentieth-century dictators. In 1909, Nicaraguan President José Santos Zelaya threatened to seize U.S. mining interests and nationalize them — take them over in the name of the nation. The U.S. government encouraged Nicaraguans to rise up against the Zelaya government, and they did. Zelaya was overthrown. In 1912, U.S. troops were dispatched to the country to protect U.S. property. That same year, the United States helped install Adolfo Diaz as president. Diaz, who governed Nicaragua in dictatorial fashion, was an enthusiastic backer of U.S. policy there. He was also a former employee of one of the U.S. mining companies in Nicaragua.

U.S. troops stayed in Nicaragua for the next thirteen years. In 1925 they left briefly, but unrest broke out again, and back they came. On this occasion, the rebel leader they were assigned to destroy was Augusto César Sandino. In 1934, Sandino was murdered on orders from Anastasio Somoza, a Nicaraguan soldier who had received his military training from U.S. officers. At about the same time,

Somoza became dictator. For the next forty-five years, he and his family held Nicaragua in the grip of terror.

The United States has helped bring other dictators to power in Latin America. In 1954, the Central Intelligence Agency encouraged Guatemalans to rebel against their elected president, Jacobo Arbenz Guzmán. (Like many people in Spanish-speaking nations, Arbenz Guzmán had two last names. He was known by the first of them, Arbenz.) U.S. officials defended their actions against Arbenz on the grounds that he was a communist. Arbenz had bought weapons from Czechoslovakia, a communist nation, they pointed out.

But according to many in Latin America, there was more than an objection to Czech guns behind the CIA-backed rebellion. Arbenz had announced plans to nationalize four million acres of land that belonged to the United Fruit Company. In 1954, the company was not using that land for growing crops, but company officials said they would one day need it for a banana plantation. Arbenz had no right to deprive them of their property, they protested.

In the end, United Fruit kept its acreage. The rebels were victorious, and Arbenz fled the country. Since 1954, Guatemala has been governed by dictators friendly to the United States. Their rule has been brutal, so brutal that in 1977, Congress voted to stop sending U.S. aid to the country.

That is not quite the end of what Latin Americans have to say about the insurrection in Guatemala. In 1954, they remind us, the U.S. secretary of state was John Foster Dulles. Earlier, Dulles had been a member of the law firm that represented United Fruit in Guatemala. One of his assistants at the State Department was a stockholder in the company. His brother, Allen Dulles, was head of the CIA in 1954. Allen Dulles was a former president of United Fruit.

U.S. officials, unlike many in Latin America, usually dismiss the government–United Fruit link as meaningless. The United States was genuinely concerned about a communist threat in Guatemala in 1954, they say. They add that other events in Latin America confirm this country's unselfish motives. Consider, for example, the fact that the United States helped Cuba and Puerto Rico win their freedom from Spain, and Panama its independence from Colombia.

Here again, Latins see things differently. The United States did not want a truly free Cuba and Puerto Rico and a truly free Panama, they say, but a Cuba, Puerto Rico, and Panama willing to do whatever this country wanted them to do. After all, Puerto Rico actually became a U.S. possession. Part of Panama, the Canal Zone, was virtually a U.S. colony. So, in many ways, was Cuba.

Three years after the Spanish-American War of 1898, Congress passed the Platt Amendment. This piece of legislation was named for Orville Platt, the senator who sponsored it. Under the Platt Amendment, Cuba could not make treaties with other countries without the consent of the United States. It could not borrow money without U.S. permission, either. The amendment gave the United States a permanent military base at Cuba's Guantánamo Bay. This country still occupies that base today. The Platt Amendment also stated that the United States could, at any time, intervene in Cuban affairs in order to preserve its independence and to maintain law and order. Not until 1933 did the United States abrogate — get rid of — the Platt Amendment.

As far as Latin Americans are concerned, the U.S. role in Panama's break with Colombia was suspect, too. The United States encouraged the Panama revolt, not from love of liberty, but from a desire to get the land for its Central American canal. A U.S. warship off the Panama coast prevented Colombian troops from landing and putting down the uprising.

"I took the canal," President Theodore Roosevelt boasted. He — and the United States — had. Like Cuba, Panama was not really free. In the Canal Zone, a ten-mile-wide strip of land across the middle of the country, the United States was supreme. Panama signed a treaty giving this country "all rights, power and authority within the zone." And the treaty gave the United States those rights in perpetuity — forever.

"I took the canal." To Latin ears, Roosevelt's words rang with arrogance. The United States had wanted a canal zone and the United States had snatched one. Panamanians had no real say in the matter. Colombian rights were utterly ignored.

This was not the only occasion upon which President Roosevelt spoke insultingly of Latin America and of its people. He was furious when word came from Bogotá, Colombia's capital, that the government had turned down his offer to buy land for the canal. "I do not think that Bogotá lot of jack rabbits should be allowed permanently to bar one of the future highways of civilization," he wrote. The next year, in issuing the Roosevelt corollary to the Monroe Doctrine, the president spoke of "chronic wrongdoing" by some Latin nations. His words made the people of those nations sound like naughty children. And if, as Roosevelt said, "civilized nations" should correct the wrongdoing, what did that make the Latin republics? Uncivilized?

Roosevelt regularly referred to Latin Americans as "dagos." He once labeled the nations of Central America and the Caribbean "small bandit nests of a wicked and inefficient type." Even the Cubans with whom Roosevelt and his Rough Riders fought in 1898 came in for his scathing criticism. They were "that cheating mañana lot." The idea that Latin Americans are childlike and lazy, always happy to postpone serious action until mañana — tomorrow — is a prejudice that many in the United States shared, and continue to share today.

Roosevelt's conviction that the United States is superior, Latin America inferior, has been held by many in this country. Calling such nations as Guatemala and Honduras "banana republics" is hardly respectful to the people who live there. Even President Franklin Roosevelt, Latin America's "good neighbor," could be condescending at times. "They think they are as good as we are," Franklin Roosevelt once said of Latin Americans, "and many of them are." More recently, U.S. Secretary of State Henry Kissinger spoke slightingly of Latin America in a conversation with the foreign minister of Chile. "Nothing important can come from the South," Kissinger told the Chilean during the 1970s. "What happens in the South is of no importance."

How do such attitudes square with this country's efforts to create a spirit of Pan-Americanism? To a great many Latin Americans, they square very well. They say that Pan-Americanism has never been more than a mask, a façade. Behind it lie U.S. greed and a desire to stand alone as the world's most powerful nation.

It is true that Pan-Americanism and U.S. trade have long been linked. The first Pan-American conference in 1889 was planned by Secretary of State James G. Blaine, the same man who called trade with Latin America the United States' "especial province."

Over the years, Latin Americans complain, the United States has dominated Pan-American conferences. The United States has pushed for trade agreements favorable to its interests. Reluctantly, Latin America has gone along. But when Latin delegates to the meetings press for arrangements that will benefit their economies, the United States refuses to listen. This U.S. habit of ignoring Latin America's needs and concerns, Latin Americans say, preserves a system of "economic imperialism" in the Western Hemisphere.

The United States rejects this idea. Imperialism, in the U.S. view, means the political domination of one land by another. Imperialism was what the Spanish and Portuguese empire builders began practicing in the New World five hundred years ago. It is what the Soviet Union practices today in Poland, Hungary, and the other communist dictatorships of Eastern Europe — and what the Soviets will practice in Latin America, too, if they can get away with it.

"Economic imperialism," on the other hand, does not exist as far as the United States is concerned. The United States has investments in Latin America, certainly. But there is nothing imperialistic about the private citizens of one country owning property in another country. It is purely a matter of business.

Those who defend the United States against a charge of economic imperialism point out that in this century, the United States has made concessions to Latin American governments. In the late 1930s, for instance, Bolivia and Mexico announced takeovers of various United States oil properties. Earlier, the U.S. government might have sent in troops to seize back the property, but President Franklin Roosevelt ordered no such invasion. A peaceful settlement was reached, with the Latin nations repaying the oil companies for their losses. Doesn't that prove that there is no such thing as economic imperialism in U.S.–Latin American relations?

It proves nothing of the kind, Latin Americans respond. After all, Bolivia and Mexico paid for what they took. Besides, the agreements included other concessions that paved the way for even more profitable U.S. investment in Latin America.

The Roosevelt administration had another reason for settling the oil disputes peacefully, Latins contend. By the late 1930s, World War II was clearly about to begin. When it did, Roosevelt wanted the Americas to stand united against the enemy. He had no intention of angering the Latin nations, nor of doing anything that might provoke any of them into fighting on the side of Germany and Japan. Maintaining friendly relations with Latin America was part of Roosevelt's war strategy, many believed.

If they were right, the strategy worked — but only

just. All Latin America did eventually join in the U.S. war effort. Brazil and Mexico even sent troops to take an active part in the fighting. But several countries were reluctant to declare war. One, Argentina, did not take that step until March 1945, a few months before the war ended.

It is no coincidence that a month after Argentina declared war, the first United Nations conference was held in San Francisco. Membership in the organization was to be limited to nations that had gone to war against Germany or Japan. And UN membership appeared attractive to Argentina and to the other Latin American nations. In such a world body, their views could be expressed, their voices heard. In the United Nations, they thought, they would at last be able to deal with the United States on equal terms.

As it turned out, they were wrong. There was to be no equality. The United States was too powerful, and the Latin nations too weak. Latin America is fully represented in the United Nations' 157-member General Assembly. But its nations were denied a permanent seat on the smaller and more important Security Council. The council has five permanent members — the United States, Britain, France, the Soviet Union, and China. It also has ten seats that are open to nations on a revolving basis. Latin America occupies two of these seats. Latin Americans are convinced that the United States used its influence to keep them from winning a permanent place on the Security Council. This has added to their resentment of their northern neighbor.

The resentment extends to the Organization of American States. Even in this regional group, Latin Americans say, the United States dominates. "The OAS should be thoroughly recast," asserts Salvador de Madariaga, a Spanish writer. Actually, Madariaga is convinced that Latin America's best future lies in firm alliances with this country. But in his view, the alliances that exist today are not fair. "There is a fundamental make-believe" in the OAS, Madariaga says, "in that it is supposed to be a meeting of equal partners on equal terms, while in fact the U.S.A. dominates the whole."

The dissatisfaction many Latin Americans feel with the OAS has to do with the purpose of the alliance and what it aims to accomplish. The United States, they say, sees the OAS primarily as a means of resisting aggression — communist aggression. But Latin Americans would like to see the organization used to help their nations solve their social and economic problems. Like earlier generations of Latin Americans who felt that the United States was using Pan-Americanism to promote its trade, many in Latin America today believe that this country uses the OAS to pursue its global quarrels with the Soviet Union. The quarrels go on and on, and Latin hopes and aspirations are always getting lost in the shuffle, they say.

Yet once, it seemed as if the United States were going to put Latin America's needs first. In March 1961, President John F. Kennedy called for an "Alliance for Progress" between the United States and Latin America. As Kennedy described it, the alliance would enable the people of the American republics to leave their feudal way of life behind them at last.

The alliance was intended to be a self-help program. It called for the United States to provide Latin America with close to $20 billion over ten years. The money would be used to achieve specific goals: raising incomes, increasing food supplies, improving public health, making land available to the landless. For their part, the Latin countries would agree to spend the money wisely and make sure it was doing the most permanent good to the greatest number of people.

Latin enthusiasm for the alliance was matched only by Latin disappointment when it failed. Congress did vote some money for the program, but not nearly what Kennedy had asked for. Much of the amount it did agree to spend went to Latin America as loans rather than gifts. Latin America got less money than it needed — and a growing debt it did not need at all. At the end of ten years, say Latin analysts, not one of the alliance's goals had been met.

As the 1970s began, economic conditions were even worse than they had been in 1961.

But by then, no one in the United States was paying much attention to the alliance's failure. This country was looking at other developments. For the event that the United States had long feared had come to pass. One of Latin America's nations had fallen under the influence of a European power. Cuba had become communist.

5

Communism
in Latin America:
A Rising Tide?

As far as the public was concerned, the Cuban missile crisis began on October 22, 1962. At seven
o'clock that evening, President John Kennedy appeared on television to announce that the Soviet
Union was arming Cuba with nuclear weapons. The
Soviets must stop their work at once, Kennedy
warned. If they did not, the United States might be
forced to stop it for them — with a nuclear blast.
Horrified, the world waited for the Soviets to react.

Although the crisis came as a surprise to the public, it had been building up for months. In 1958,
Cuban rebels overthrew the harsh government of
dictator Fulgencio Batista y Zaldívar. Batista fled,
leaving Cuba to the rebels and to their leader, Fidel
Castro Ruz.

Castro was a charismatic leader in the Latin manner. His black beard and rough appearance con-
trasted dramatically with his university education
and his gift for fiery speechmaking. Even before he
assumed the office of premier on February 16, Dr.

Castro was turning his rhetorical talents against the United States.

Cuba had never known freedom, he charged. After four hundred years as a Spanish possession, the Platt Amendment of 1901 practically turned the island into a colony of the United States. The amendment was abrogated in 1933, but Cuba's status hardly changed. United States citizens — "Yankee imperialists," Castro called them — continued to own and control the country's main source of wealth, its sugar cane plantations and sugar mills. Through the years, the great majority of Cubans were bound, feudal-fashion, to labor on Yankee sugar properties. Or so Castro told his people.

Although the United States made overtures of friendship to the new government, Castro rejected them. His anti–United States tirades became more virulent. Before long, this country was responding in kind. U.S. leaders pointed out that Castro, like Batista, had made himself absolute dictator. They also suspected him of harboring communist sympathies. Soon, they were saying that Castro actually was a communist. They warned that if he went ahead with plans to nationalize Cuban industries the United States might stop buying Cuban sugar altogether. Since this country was Cuba's principal customer, such a boycott could devastate the Cuban economy.

Castro ignored the threat and began nationalization. He also started taking over the country's huge estates. This land was not handed over to individual Cubans, but was held, communist-style, by the government in the name of the people. Angered by the trend toward communism, the United States announced that it was no longer in the market for Cuban sugar.

But Castro already had another buyer — the Soviet Union. That country quickly replaced the United States as Cuba's main trading partner. The Soviets also offered Castro loans and gifts of money to build his nation's economy. They sent in military equipment and helped Cubans construct roads and airfields. By early 1961, the Cuban-Soviet alliance seemed firm.

It seemed dangerous, too. A communist nation just ninety miles from the United States mainland posed a real threat to our security, many believed.

One danger was that the Soviets might install nuclear weapons in Cuba. Soviet missiles there would be capable of reaching and destroying cities across the United States. Another danger had to do with Cuba's location in the Caribbean Sea. The Panama Canal opens into that sea. Whoever controls the Caribbean is in a position to control the canal. Looking ahead, U.S. officials could envision a day when Castro and his friends in Moscow might prevent passage of U.S. ships between the Atlantic and the Pacific. Nearly half of all U.S. foreign trade follows that route. But of the dangers involved in

Cuba's turn toward communism, the one that seemed most frightening to people in the United States was this: It might be only the beginning.

The Soviets have never hidden their conviction that the communist way of life is superior to any other and that many nations will eventually adopt it. What if they began using Cuba as a staging point from which to launch a drive to impose their system through the Americas? Where would we be then?

U.S. leaders decided not to wait to find out. By 1960, top officials of this country's CIA were plotting to get rid of Castro once and for all. In 1961, when Kennedy became president, the officials filled him in on the details.

The scheme called for invading Cuba. The actual invaders would be about fifteen hundred anti-Castro Cubans then living in Florida. But the blueprint for the invasion had been drawn up by CIA agents. The CIA was also paying for it and promising that U.S. planes would provide the invaders with air cover if necessary. Once ashore, the invading forces would get in touch with anti-communists inside Cuba. CIA officials told the president they were positive that thousands would rally to overthrow the Castro regime. Members of the Cuban army would join the rebels as well, the U.S. secret agents predicted. Although President Kennedy had some doubts about the plan, he agreed to go ahead with it.

Early in the morning of April 17, 1961, the operation got under way. It took place on Cuba's marshy south coast at a spot known as Bahia de los Cochinos — the Bay of Pigs.

The Bay of Pigs invasion was over within hours. The CIA had miscalculated; anti-Castro Cubans did not rise to support it, and Cuban troops remained loyal. Most of the invaders were captured. The CIA's bold plan crumbled into a humiliating defeat for the United States.

For Castro, though, it was a triumph — and a vindication of his anti–United States views. Here was proof that the United States was determined to keep Cuba under its thumb, he said. For its own safety, Cuba must move even further away from the United States and closer to the Soviet Union. The next December, Castro formally announced that his revolution was a "Marxist-Leninist" one. That meant he, and Cuba, were definitely in the communist camp. Karl Marx was one of the first to write about the theory of communism. Vladimir Lenin helped establish communism in Russia after that country's 1917 revolution.

The strengthening of the Cuban-Soviet alliance brought the world one step closer to the Cuban missile crisis. Another step came seven months later. In July 1962, cameras aboard United States spy planes flying over the island photographed missile pads under construction there. Intelligence officers began watching for signs of actual missiles and their deadly warheads.

By October, those signs were apparent. A fleet of twenty-five ships was headed toward Cuba. In the past, the Soviets had used similar ships to transport nuclear weapons. Were they doing so again? The United States could take no chances. President Kennedy took to the airwaves.

Never would the Soviets unload warheads in Cuban ports, he asserted. The United States would blockade the island, even if that meant firing on Soviet ships. If a single missile was launched from Cuba, this country would respond with a full-scale nuclear attack upon the Soviet Union itself.

For forty-eight hours, the world waited, hovering fearfully on the brink of nuclear holocaust. Then the Soviets made their decision. On October 24, the ships turned back. Two days after that, the Soviet government agreed to dismantle the missile sites. In return, Kennedy promised that the United States would never sponsor another anti-Castro Cuban invasion. The immediate crisis was over.

But the long-term problem was not. Cuba was still communist and friendlier than ever with the Soviet superpower. And now, Castro was doing something else that the United States had long feared he might do. He was promising to "export" Cuba's revolution and to encourage communist uprisings in other nations.

Here was a new challenge to the Monroe Doctrine. That doctrine had slipped into relative disuse since 1933. Franklin Roosevelt's Good Neighbor policy had discouraged U.S. interference in Latin affairs. Now, however, many thought it high time to trot the doctrine out again — and update it into the bargain.

Originally, the doctrine sought to keep foreign imperialists out of the Americas. Later, it was modified to prohibit European diplomatic interference in New World affairs and, later still, to allow the United States to intervene in Latin matters in order to prevent other countries from intervening first. But the kind of aggression the nations of the Western Hemisphere faced from modern communism was different from all earlier threats, many believed. It was beyond the scope of the Monroe Doctrine to deal with.

The Dominican Republic provided a case in point. As we know, the United States took over Dominican finances in 1905 and ran them until 1941. During eight years of that time, from 1916 to 1924, U.S. troops occupied the Caribbean nation militarily. In 1930, with U.S. backing, Rafael Trujillo Molina became dictator there. In 1961, after a cruel thirty-one-year rule, Trujillo was assassinated. Elections were held, and a liberal named Juan Bosch became president.

A year later, in 1963, Bosch was ousted in a coup and a new dictatorship imposed. In April 1965, supporters of Bosch rebelled against that dictatorship. Civil war broke out.

By then, Lyndon B. Johnson was president of the United States. To him, the Dominican civil war seemed to threaten disaster. Intelligence reports indicated that some communists might have infiltrated the Bosch forces. What if those forces won the civil war? The communists among them might seize power in a new government. The Dominican Republic would be a "second Cuba."

Johnson was determined to prevent that. On April 28, he ordered twenty thousand U.S. troops into the country. Within hours, the fighting was over. The next July, Joaquin Balaguer became president. Balaguer was a long-time political ally of former dictator Trujillo.

How did President Johnson justify invading the Dominican Republic? The country's civil war was an internal affair. There had been no hint of foreign imperialism, diplomatic meddling, or intervention. If the Dominican Republic had become a "second Cuba," it would not have been because of direct attack from any outside force. It would have been because of communists within the Bosch forces.

But the very fact that those communists existed was in itself proof of intervention from outside, Johnson and his advisers argued. The infiltration of communists into the pro-Bosch alliance did not just happen. It had been planned, planned by shrewd and skillful communist agents in Havana and Moscow. Thus, a civil war that seemed to be a private matter was actually no such thing. The fighting in the Dominican Republic, Johnson was convinced, was the direct result of outside communist influence.

From here, it was only a short step to justifying intervention. Back in 1823, President Monroe had told Congress that no one "can . . . believe that our southern brethren, if left to themselves would adopt [rule by a foreign power] of their own accord." President Johnson certainly couldn't believe it. Left to themselves, he was sure, the Dominicans would have demanded assistance in ending the war. The argument seemed convincing enough in Washington, D.C. The Monroe Doctrine could be used against internal communist agitation, as well as against outright foreign attack.

In the months that followed, U.S. troops in the Dominican Republic were gradually joined by, and some of them replaced by, soldiers from several Latin nations. These nations acted at the urging of the United States, under an OAS mutual-defense treaty. Fifteen months after the invasion, and about a month after Balaguer took over, all the OAS troops left.

Over the years, the United States has kept a wary eye on communist activity elsewhere in the Latin world. Brazil's government fought a war against leftist rebels between 1966 and 1975. The government, a right-wing military one, emerged the victor. It ruled harshly for ten years, until 1985, when a civilian president took over.

In Chile, the communist "attack" came by means of the ballot box. Chileans elected a Marxist, Salvador Allende Gossens, president in 1970. President Allende nationalized industry and began breaking up the huge *haciendas* of Chile's wealthy landowners — but not for long. He was killed in 1973, during the course of a military coup. Many people in Chile, and in the United States, suspected that this coup was carried out with the approval of the U.S. Central Intelligence Agency. Chile's new president, General Augusto Pinochet Ugarte, was a strong anticommunist. He pledged to remain dictator until at least 1989.

Events in Chile did not stop the communists, however. In 1979, Nicaragua became the second Latin country to adopt a Marxist form of government. On July 16 of that year, rebels forced Nicaraguan president Luis Anastasio Somoza Debayle from office. Somoza was the son of the Anastasio Somoza who had imposed a harsh dictatorship upon Nicaragua in the 1930s. As we know, the first Somoza gained power with the help of the United States. He seized control in Nicaragua and ordered the murder of the leftist leader Augusto Sandino. Recalling that killing, and regarding Sandino as a hero, the rebels who overthrew the second Somoza called themselves Sandinistas.

During the months that the Sandinistas were winning their revolution, the president of the United States was Jimmy Carter. Unlike President Johnson during the Dominican uprising of 1965, Carter did not interfere in Nicaragua. Unlike Johnson — and unlike virtually all other presidents before him — Carter questioned whether the United States had the right to intervene at will in Latin America.

In fact, President Carter actually welcomed the Sandinista revolution in some ways. He regarded the overthrow of the Somoza dictatorship as a victory for human rights and social justice. Human rights were very important to Jimmy Carter. Throughout his four years in office, he made a policy of encouraging repressive governments around the world to free political prisoners and guarantee certain freedoms to their people. Thousands of men and women in Latin America today believe they owe their lives to Carter's human rights policies. Although many in the United States criticized Carter for his tacit support of the Sandinistas, the president pointed out that they had promised to introduce democracy to Nicaragua. Carter accepted that promise, in the beginning, at least. Later he realized that democracy might be a long time coming to Nicaragua.

Their revolution won, the Sandinistas settled

down to govern through a three-member *junta*. Chief spokesman for the *junta* was Daniel Ortega Saavedra. Behind Ortega and the *junta* stood a nine-member National Directorate.

Like Castro in Cuba and Allende in Chile, Ortega and the Sandinistas were determined to change their country's political and economic systems. During their first four years in power, they claimed, the percentage of Nicaraguans who owned land jumped from two to sixty-two. Health care improved. Citizens, allowed no voice in government during the Somoza regime, were permitted to speak out at public meetings with members of the directorate. A presidential election was scheduled for 1984.

Long before it could take place, relations between Nicaragua and the United States changed drastically. In 1980, President Carter ran for re-election. His opponent was Ronald W. Reagan. Reagan won the election and was inaugurated in January.

The new president held social and political convictions very different from those of his predecessor. To him, the communist takeover in Nicaragua was a calamity. Reagan was one of those who thought Carter had been wrong to offer moral support to the Sandinistas. In his view, that support had opened the door to another Soviet conquest in the Western Hemisphere. And Ronald Reagan distrusted the Soviet Union intensely. It was an "evil empire," he said. Rather than allow the Sandinista victory, Reagan believed, Carter should have given Somoza the military assistance he needed to stay in power. A concern for human rights was all very well, but preventing the spread of communism in Latin America was even more urgent.

Not that human rights had been served by the Sandinista victory anyway, Reagan added. In his opinion, the communists were making life worse, not better, for their people. They were turning Nicaragua into a "totalitarian dungeon." His point of view was shared by others. One Reagan administration official referred to Sandinista Nicaragua as "an infected piece of meat" attracting "insects" to it.

The Sandinista land reform program was a fraud, this official, and others, believed. They were not giving land directly to the people, but were, in the way of communists, seizing it in the name of the state. Nor were they offering political freedom. The Nicaraguan press was censored. Citizens were allowed to speak with members of the directorate, but few who did so dared utter a word of criticism. Dissenters ran the risk of prison. The 1984 elections were sure to be unfair and undemocratic.

Worst of all though, Reagan administration officials said, the Sandinistas were trying to foment revolution in other Latin nations. And they were doing so, the officials added, on direct orders from Cuba and the Soviet Union.

6

To Stem the Tide: Central America and the Caribbean

In 1979, civil war broke out in El Salvador, Nicaragua's neighbor to the northwest. On one side was the nation's ruling military *junta;* on the other, thousands of left-wing revolutionaries. The fighting was the culmination of nearly a decade of unrest and rioting. Communism, Ronald Reagan said, was on the move again.

Five years later, Reagan was in the fourth year of his presidency and the Salvadoran war was still going on. By then, the rebels controlled about a third of the countryside, although cities and major roads and airports remained in government hands. From time to time, the leftists managed to destroy a bridge or blow up a power station, but government forces usually repaired the damage quickly.

Repairing damage is one thing, however, and winning a war is another. The Salvadoran army, strong though it might be in the cities, could not find and defeat the rebels in the country areas where they hid out, seeking shelter with sympathetic farmers and peasants. If it was going to crush the leftists once and for all, the army needed help. To President Reagan, believing as he did that the Soviet Union was an evil empire that the United States must stand up to around the world, there seemed only one possible course of action. The United States must defend El Salvador's government.

So this country once again became involved in a Latin American civil war. By the end of 1982, 52 U.S. military officers were in El Salvador. Within two years, that number had risen to about 160. At least 55 of the officers were military advisers, whose assignment was helping the Salvadoran government and army devise strategies for overpowering the rebels. Marine security guards, army medics, and supervisors — close to 100 in all — made up the rest of the official U.S. presence. Unofficially, as many as 150 CIA agents may have been working against the leftists.

As the number of U.S. personnel in El Salvador rose, so did military aid to the country. In 1979, the United States had given the Salvadoran government only $4000 in military grants and loans. The next year, President Carter raised that to $6 million. The year after that, the first year of President Reagan's term of office, the figure reached $35 million. For 1985, Reagan told Congress $311 million would be needed.

Much of the money has gone for equipment.

Thanks to the United States, the Salvadoran military has airplanes and helicopters, howitzers, rifles, grenade launchers, anti-aircraft guns, patrol boats, and much more. The United States has used other funds to make its own troops and military hardware available to the Salvadorans. U.S. pilots have flown reconnaissance missions over the jungle highlands where the rebels find cover. Ships of the U.S. Navy have been stationed offshore to intercept rebel messages. The U.S. training and advisory programs have cost millions, too, as have CIA operations.

Along with its military assistance, the United States announced its intention of enabling El Salvador to establish a stable working democracy. Like most other Latin nations, El Salvador has little experience with representative government. During much of the twentieth century, its government has been controlled by dictators. Its press has been censored, and its "elections" have been marred by fraud and violence.

In May 1984, however, El Salvador did hold an honest election — its first in fifty years. At least, that was what United States officials claimed, and they should know. This country played a leading part in planning and running the election. It contributed $2 million — maybe more — to the campaign of the candidate favored by the Reagan administration. That candidate was José Napoleón Duarte. When the election was over, Duarte was declared the winner.

But it takes more than an election to make a democracy. One hallmark of a democratic nation is that its civilian leaders command its military organizations. That's the way it is in countries like the United States, Canada, and England and in Costa Rica and Belize. In El Salvador, it has been different. No civilian government there has been able to control the military. Consequently, army officers — most of them conservatives — have run the country pretty much as they pleased, crushing any sign of opposition or dissent.

Opposition has not had to be left-wing to run afoul of the military. Most members of the Salvadoran army have considered even democratic ideas — such as the idea of holding free elections or of redistributing land to individual peasants — as unacceptable. To keep such ideas from being discussed and to terrorize dissenters into keeping silent, army officers and government leaders organized private "death squads."

Composed of small groups of officers and soldiers, the death squads became instruments in a campaign of terror by the Salvadoran government. Between 1979 and 1984, the squads kidnapped, tortured, and murdered by the thousands. According to human rights groups, as many as forty thousand men and women may have been killed by government forces during those years. Hundreds of bodies, many of them mutilated, have been found. Other death squad victims have simply disappeared. They are known as *desaparecidos,* "disappeared ones." Many of the dead and disappeared have been in their teens and early twenties. Most have been Salvadoran, although in 1980, members of one squad killed four women from the United States. The four, three of whom were nuns, had been working at a Catholic Church mission. Death squads also murdered two U.S. agricultural advisers in 1981.

To many in this country, it appeared that the Salvadoran government's most important job was to eliminate the squads and get control of the military. In fact, Congress made that one condition for sending more aid to the country. In 1981, members of the Senate and the House of Representatives agreed to suspend assistance if President Reagan could not assure them that the Salvadoran government was disbanding the death squads and moving toward protecting the rights of all citizens.

In the months just before Duarte's election, the number of killings did drop. Fifty-eight civilians were murdered in February 1984; forty-six, the next month. In June, only eleven deaths were reported. What's more, five members of one death squad finally were brought to trial for the murders of the U.S. churchwomen. All were found guilty.

That was good news. In September, U.S. Secretary of State George P. Shultz sent Congress a statement "certifying" Duarte's progress toward creating a true democracy. His government "has demonstrated continued progress on ... the termination of death-squad activities," Shultz reported.

At the same time, the secretary of state informed Congress that Duarte was reforming his country in other ways. A land redistribution program was going well. Duarte was also establishing law and order, Shultz wrote, rebuilding the judicial system and allowing Salvadorans more political freedom.

Certified progress toward democracy plus increased U.S. military aid to the government. Would they add up to quick defeat for the rebels? Unfortunately not, Reagan administration officials admitted. The reason: The rebels still had all the resources of the international communist movement at their command.

Earlier, in May 1984, Reagan had spoken to the nation on television, spelling out exactly the route communist resources had taken on their way to El Salvador. "Weapons, supplies and funds are shipped from the Soviet bloc to Cuba, from Cuba to Nicaragua, from Nicaragua to the Salvadoran guerrillas," he said. "These facts were confirmed last year."

In the president's mind, this left him no choice. The supplies must be stopped — interdicted. Until they were, he warned, the fighting would continue.

But trying to interdict the shipments by seizing each one as it was smuggled over the Nicaragua–El Salvador border was not going to do the trick. In that dense mountainous jungle, many loads would slip past even the most watchful eyes. Instead, the president said, the communists must be persuaded to abandon their supply program altogether. They must be kept too busy to have any time to devote to helping the Salvadoran rebels. To Reagan, keeping them busy meant continuing to pursue the CIA's so-called "covert" war in Nicaragua.

At first, the CIA war really was a secret. In 1981, Reagan approved a $19 million plan to harass the Sandinistas and undermine their government. U.S. agents began meeting with Nicaraguan opponents of that government.

A few of the dissidents were Miskito Indians from the nothern part of the country. The Miskitos told horror stories of persecution by Sandinista death squads known as *turbas*. Others were former Sandinistas who had deserted the party when they saw it abandoning its promise of a free press and democratic reforms. But by far the largest number of anti-Sandinista Nicaraguans were members of ex-dictator Anastasio Somoza's National Guard. Their goal was to restore right-wing government in their country.

Although the anti-Sandinistas represented a wide variety of political points of view, that fact was seldom mentioned. The CIA generally lumped all of them together as *contras*. *Contra* is the Spanish word for "against."

Months passed, and the secret meetings between *contras* and CIA agents continued. By 1984, the agency had spent $73 million to destabilize the Sandinistas. The *contras* were becoming well supplied with sophisticated weapons and equipment. They were also carrying out successful raids against various targets within Nicaragua. In the fall of 1983, they destroyed two major oil storage depots. The next spring, explosive mines were detonated in Nicaraguan harbors. Six Nicaraguan ships were damaged.

The harbor mining brought the CIA's covert war fully into the open. The agency revealed that it had planned and financed the operation. The secret war was no secret anymore.

Or so people thought at the time. Within weeks, though, they were hearing about a second secret war in Central America.

The soldiers in this war were United States citizens, many of them veterans of the war in Vietnam. The United States undertook that war in the 1960s in an attempt to keep the Southeast Asian nation of South Vietnam from becoming communist. The effort failed and a communist government took over in South Vietnam after the United States withdrew its forces in 1973. A few of the war's disappointed U.S.

survivors returned home anxious to put their battle skills to use against communism in other parts of the world. They became professional soldiers — mercenaries. Mercenaries fight for pay, hiring themselves out wherever a war may be going on.

Late in 1984, it was unclear exactly how many U.S. mercenaries were in Latin America, planning and leading commando raids, flying reconnaissance planes, ferrying arms and supplies to anticommunist forces. Some figures were available, however. A United States–based private military organization called Civilian Military Assistance announced that about fifteen of its members were in Nicaragua. The editor and publisher of *Soldier of Fortune,* a magazine for mercenaries, said he had dispatched about ten specifically trained twelve-man teams there as well. Other organizations may have sent other fighters. The U.S. public had no way of knowing for sure.

The U.S. government, on the other hand, probably knew precisely the strength of the second undercover force in Central America. Questioned by reporters, officials at the United States embassy in San Salvador, the capital of El Salvador, acknowledged that they were aware of what the mercenaries were doing. One U.S. military officer in El Salvador had express orders to act as liaison between the mercenaries and the Salvadorans.

The U.S. government was encouraging other forms of private aid to Central America's anticommunists. In 1984, about 1.5 million dollars' worth of privately collected goods and supplies was reaching the *contras* each month. Much of it was coming from such organizations as the Christian Broadcasting Network, the Committee for the Survival of a Free Congress, the Conservative Caucus, and *Soldier of Fortune* magazine. Working with the U.S. Department of State and the White House, these groups sought donations of money, medicine, food, and uniforms from businesses and corporations. The supplies were stored at government facilities, including Fort Meade in Maryland and an Air National Guard base in Selfridge, Michigan. Air Force planes were transporting the goods to Central America.

By the summer of 1984, the private aid was proving a substantial help to their cause, administration officials agreed. It was allowing the CIA to save money on civilian goods and to concentrate its spending on weapons. Without the private help, the attempt to keep the Sandinistas off balance might have been hampered by a shortage of funds.

The United States' anti-Sandinista campaign had other facets. One was an economic boycott. Starting in 1981, this country refused to sell certain goods to the Sandinistas. Soon, Nicaraguans were desperately short of food, cooking oil, gasoline, soap, and toilet paper, among other items. One Sandinista official estimated that by 1985, the United States had inflicted a loss of $1.1 billion upon his country. Not satisfied with this, the Reagan administration announced new restrictions on trade with Nicaragua in April 1985.

Another part of the effort to weaken the Sandinistas involved widening the war against them. Just as this country's fight against Salvadoran leftists had led to its undertaking the secret war against Nicaragua, so that war impelled it to carry the military effort into other, neighboring Central American nations.

In Honduras, the United States began constructing base camps for the *contras*. Honduras has had a civilian government since 1981, but military officials still control the country from behind the scenes. At the newly constructed Honduran camps are living quarters, dining facilities, hospitals, and administration buildings. Here the *contras* could live safely while receiving training from U.S. officers. From here, they could launch their raids across the border into Nicaragua. Here, too, the United States could take charge of training the Honduran army. By 1984, half of that ten-thousand-man force was United States–trained. This country spent a total of $83 million in Honduras in 1982 and 1983.

But the most obvious and dramatic evidence of U.S. military activity in and around Honduras came between August 1983 and February 1984. It was called Big Pine II.

The government described Big Pine II as a routine

training exercise. Actually, Big Pine II was "probably the longest military exercise ever." This description came from the Center for Defense Information. The center, based in Washington, D.C., keeps tabs on military planning and spending. Its director, Gene R. LaRocque, is a former rear admiral in the U.S. Navy. Military experts at the center point out that a "routine" military exercise lasts a few days or weeks, not six months.

Big Pine II was unusual in other ways, too. At its peak, six thousand U.S. troops were in Honduras. When it ended, one thousand stayed behind. Ordinarily, when a military exercise ends, those who took part in it go home. Big Pine II was also more elaborate than exercises normally are. It was expensive, too, costing more than $75 million.

The U.S. show of strength and its military build-up went beyond Honduras to other Central American nations. One was Guatemala. As we saw, Congress had cut off military aid to that nation's brutal government back in 1977. Nevertheless, Guatemala continued to buy military equipment from private U.S. suppliers. Now, President Reagan was encouraging those suppliers to increase their sales. By the mid-1980s, millions of dollars' worth of helicopters, rifles, machine guns, jeeps, and riot-control equipment had made their way to Guatemala.

Military assistance also went to Panama. There, where this country had its Canal Zone to protect, nine thousand U.S. troops were stationed. To accommodate this force, the United States was maintaining eighteen separate military facilities, one as headquarters for the United States Southern Command — Southcom. According to the Center for Defense Information, Southcom's staff grew from 178 in 1981 to more than 300 in 1984. It operated twenty-nine Military Training teams in 1981, ninety-four just three years later. "We're putting our best soldiers into Southcom," one administration official said with satisfaction.

In the future, the U.S. military presence in Panama may be reduced. Under a 1978 treaty worked out between President Carter and Panamanian leaders, the Canal Zone will be returned to Panama in 1999. Until then, though, the United States can be expected to keep a strong force on hand there.

Costa Rica and Belize are two other Central American countries that experienced a growing involvement with the U.S. military in the 1980s. Both nations have a tradition of democracy. Both were neutral in 1984, each hoping to stay out of the fighting that has devastated so much of Central America.

But can they stay out of it? By the mid-1980s, about three thousand Nicaraguan *contras* had sought refuge in Costa Rica and started using it as a base for anti-Sandinista activity in their own land. The United States did not discourage this, though it brought conflict dangerously close to Costa Rica. In

Belize, which was the English colony British Honduras until 1981, concern focused on the possibility of war with right-wing Guatemala.

If war did come, Belize and Costa Rica would be very vulnerable. Costa Rica had only a four-thousand-person Civil Guard in 1984 and a smaller Rural Guard. Belize had a militia of eight hundred. These forces were lightly armed.

So building up the arsenals of Belize and Costa Rica became an important U.S. goal in Central America. This country granted Costa Rica $2 million for military equipment in 1982 and $2.5 million more in 1983. For 1985, President Reagan requested an increase to nearly $10 million. In Belize, military aid levels rose from $200,000 in 1982 to $600,000 in 1985.

Why the build-ups? Why the emphasis on training and equipping armies throughout Central America? Why the show of might during Big Pine II? One aim, of course, was to intimidate the Sandinistas. "Give up supplying the Salvadoran rebels, or you will have a real fight on your hands," was the message.

Another purpose can only be guessed at. One guesser was Jim Sasser, a United States senator from Tennessee. "I have seen with my own eyes a military infrastructure that could accommodate any policy decision," Sasser said after visiting Honduras in 1984. He meant that the roads, airfields, and so forth — the infrastructure — that the United States was constructing there would allow this country to launch a full-fledged war in Central America if it wished. Sasser's opinion was seconded by Lee Hamilton, a congressman from Indiana. "A group within the administration wants to win a military victory in Central America," Representative Hamilton declared.

Perhaps a group did. If so, it would not have been surprising. When Hamilton made his allegation, the Reagan administration already had one military victory under its belt in Latin America. It had come in October 1983, on the tiny Caribbean island of Grenada.

Grenada, 133 square miles in area, lies a hundred miles off the coast of Venezuela. It has about 110,000 inhabitants. For 190 years, starting in 1784, Grenada was a British colony. Independence came in 1974, and with it, trouble.

Part of the trouble was political. In a 1976 election, right-winger Eric Gairy became prime minister. For the next three years, Gairy ruled as a dictator, his decrees enforced by a death squad–like group dubbed the "Mongoose Gang."

Another part of Grenada's trouble was financial. After independence, the island's economy floundered. That, added to Gairy's harsh rule, led to rebellion. Leftists staged a coup in 1979. Their leader, Maurice Bishop, became prime minister.

Bishop's rule brought no relief. He, too, assumed

dictatorial powers and he, too, was unable to improve Grenada's economy. On October 19, 1983, Bishop himself became the victim of a coup. He was assassinated by radical leftists who quickly assumed control of the island. Grenada seemed set to align itself firmly with Cuba and the Soviet Union. Then, on October 25, U.S. Marines and Army Rangers stormed ashore.

"We have taken this decisive action for three reasons," President Reagan informed the nation as the invasion went forward.

"First, of overriding importance, to protect innocent lives, including up to one thousand Americans" — United States citizens, that is — "whose personal safety is, of course, my paramount concern." Most of these citizens — actually about seven hundred of them — were students at the island's medical school.

"Second, to forestall further chaos," the president continued. "And third, to assist in the restoration of conditions of law and order." The president contended that he had acted only after receiving "a formal request for help, a unanimous request," from other Caribbean nations. This request had come, he said, from the Organization of Eastern Caribbean States (OECS). The OECS, like the OAS, provides for mutual defense among its members.

As it turned out, Reagan later claimed a fourth reason for the invasion. U.S. troops found several hundred Cubans on the island. Many were helping to build a large modern airport near the nation's capital, St. George's.

What use did Grenada have for such an airport? administration officials demanded. The island's tourist trade is small. In fact, only 461 sleeping places are available for visitors. So why the airport — unless Cuba, Nicaragua, and the Soviet Union planned on using it as a base from which to launch fresh communist attacks on Latin America?

That was the reasoning of Reagan administration officials. Their conviction that Cuban and Soviet communists were intent upon using Grenada as a military base was re-enforced during the "mopping-up" operations that followed the invasion. Administration officials reported that caches of Cuban and Soviet weapons had been found hidden on the island.

Within days, the invaders had done their work. The young medical students were safely home. More than six thousand U.S. troops were on Grenada. Eighteen were dead, according to U.S. military officials. The same official set the number of Grenadian dead at forty-four and the Cuban toll at twenty-four. More than eleven hundred Grenadians had been arrested by U.S. military authorities. Suspecting them of left-wing sympathies, the United States was determined to keep them under lock and key.

On the whole, Grenadians seemed pleased about the invasion. Most welcomed the troops and expressed delight that they need no longer fear a communist dictatorship. Many in the United States were also enthusiastic about the president's action. Yet there were dissenting voices, as well.

7

United States Latin Policy: Does It Work?

President Ronald Reagan was exuberant about the Grenada victory. Quick decisive action had worked "to restore democratic institutions" in a land threatened by communism, he announced. To him, the moral was obvious: Similar decisive action by the United States and its allies could erase communism elsewhere in Latin America. Just let Congress vote to supply the money and the weapons and Central America would be saved. The government of El Salvador would win its victory over the leftists. The Sandinista regime would fall apart. Cuba would again be isolated, the sole Marxist nation in the hemisphere. And who knew? Castro might one day fall, too. "The people of Central America can succeed if we provide the assistance," the president assured the nation.

Others were less sure. What had worked in Grenada, where 6400 troops had overwhelmed a few hundred unprepared Cubans and Grenadians, might not work so well in larger nations where conditions were more complex and rebels numbered in the thousands, they said. But more important, it should not even be tried. The invasion of Grenada was a bad example. It was no more than old-fashioned gunboat diplomacy, the critics maintained, an illegal step backward into a shoddy interventionist past.

Illegal? The president claimed he had acted according to the treaty provisions of the OECS. But the critics responded that he had deliberately overlooked the fact that that treaty specifically prohibits any nation from meddling in the internal affairs of any other nation. And what were Bishop's assassination and the coup that preceded it but internal affairs? No evidence indicated that any outside force was involved in either. The critics also pointed out that although Reagan had said that Caribbean nations were unanimous in their demand that the United States step in in Grenada, that was not actually the case. Two countries, Trinidad and Tobago, opposed intervention. Under OECS treaty arrangements, collective action is permitted only if *all* member nations approve it.

There were other criticisms. Reagan had justified the invasion as a mission to rescue United States citizens from "great danger." But news reporters and others who talked with the students generally concluded that no such danger had truly existed. "No hard evidence has been produced to prove the threat," said an editorial in the *New York Times.* Other reasons for the invasion, Reagan said, were to put an end to "chaos" and to restore "law and order" to the island. However, by the time the troops landed, the coup was over. According to most observers, Grenada was hardly in a state of chaos by October 25.

The invasion over, administration officials added a fourth reason for having undertaken it: to rid Grenada of Cuban influences. Here, they seemed on firmer ground. What the Marines and the Rangers found as they moved across the island proved that Cubans were involved there. The airport under construction at St. George's, whether planned as a military installation or not, certainly could have doubled as one. Its restaurant space would "feed a troop movement," one U.S. witness reported. Its huge fuel storage tanks and nine-thousand-foot runway would accommodate the largest military aircraft. And the airport was being constructed largely by Cuban workers. The Cuban and Soviet weapons found on Grenada were further evidence of outside communist involvement.

But the critics didn't accept that involvement on Grenada as a justification for invasion, either. In the first place, many of the hidden weapons were so old and outdated that they would be virtually useless in modern warfare, they said. In the second, the government of Grenada surely had the right to build an

airport of whatever size and design, and using whatever labor, it wished.

In any case, the critics went on, what U.S. troops
found during the invasion was irrelevant. The rele-
vant fact was that before the invasion, this country
had no idea of the extent of the Cuban presence.
How could something the president didn't even
know about be a reason for him to order an attack?
Reagan's attempt to use the Cubans to justify his action was illogical, the critics charged, a belated attempt to make an illegal invasion appear to have had
a legitimate purpose.

Were they right? Were the reasons Reagan gave
for invading only pretexts? If so, what was the real
reason for his decision?

To critics in the United States and Latin America,
the answer seemed clear. Like many presidents before him, Reagan had seen the opportunity to overthrow a weak anti–United States government and to
replace it with a government friendly to this country.
Swiftly, and using massive military might, he had
seized that opportunity.

If the critics could have looked ahead two years
from October 1983 to October 1985, they might have
seen even more reason for believing as they did. Not
until more than a year after the invasion did Grenadians get to vote for a new government. In a December 1984 election, the leader of the recently formed
New National Party, Herbert Blaize, ran for the of-

fice of prime minister against former right-wing dictator Eric Gairy. Blaize, the candidate supported by U.S. officials, won.

But even with the election over, nearly three hundred U.S. troops remained on Grenada. Their continued presence was contrary to Reagan's October 1983 promise that all the troops would be home "by Christmas." It also violated U.S. law. After the invasion, Congress voted to require the withdrawal of the entire force within sixty days. However, the U.S. government waited until February 1985 to announce that its remaining troops were scheduled to leave the island by the next October.

The U.S. occupation force was busy during its lengthy stay on Grenada. Some of its members were there to keep the country peaceful. Others were training a new police force in sophisticated antisubversive and antiriot techniques. Still others were completing the airport at St. George's — and completing it according to its original design. When its first section opened in 1984, its dining rooms, fuel storage tanks, and runway were still of military capacity. And Grenada still had room for only 461 tourists. In the year since the invasion, the United States had spent more than $20 million to finish this modern airport. Only now, it was under U.S. control, not Cuban, and Grenada was one more piece in the anticommunist jigsaw puzzle this country was trying to assemble in Latin America.

In the days and weeks right after the invasion, of course, opponents of U.S. policy in Latin America could not have known that Grenada would remain an occupied country for so long. But already, they were growing increasingly unhappy about what President Reagan was doing throughout Central America. Many were coming to feel that the United States was too deeply involved in the fighting there. In Congress, there was a nagging worry about war.

So far, the United States was not fighting a war in Central America. The Salvadoran government and its leftist foes, the Sandinistas and the *contras,* Guatemalan, Panamanian, and Honduran armies and rebels, the civilians caught in the middle — they were the ones doing the killing and dying. The United States was just helping out, sending money, supplies, trainers, advisers, and secret agents to aid the anticommunists.

But as many members of Congress remembered, that was exactly how the United States had started out in South Vietnam twenty years before. From a few dozen trainers and advisers in the early 1960s, troop strength rose to more than half a million in 1969. Before the war ended, almost sixty thousand United States citizens had been killed. At the height of the fighting, this country was spending $40,000 a minute on the war.

Not only did the Vietnam War cost billions of dollars and thousands of lives, it proved costly at home, too. People in this country were bitterly divided over the war's morality — or lack of it. Many felt that the United States had no business trying to tell South Vietnam what kind of government it must have. Thousands of young men refused to be drafted into the army. Hundreds of thousands of civilians took to the streets to protest the fighting. In the beginning, the antiwar demonstrations were peaceful, but as the war continued, violence occasionally broke out. Only when the United States pulled out of Vietnam in 1973 did the dissent, the violence, and the bitterness die down.

Could events in Central America follow a similar course? In the early 1980s, the CIA was engaged in a war there, just as it had been in Vietnam during the early 1960s. The amount of money being spent in Central America was going up year by year, just as it had in Vietnam. The number of U.S. trainers and advisers had risen steadily in both places, too. Even as Congress worried about these similarities, Big Pine II was reaching the height of its activity. In the weeks ahead would come warnings from Senator Sasser, Representative Hamilton, and others that the United States was indeed preparing for war in Central America.

Such a war could mean more than thousands of deaths and violent dissent. If the United States did become involved in a war in Central America, Fidel Castro would surely hurl his troops into the fray.

Those troops would be outfitted with Soviet weapons. They might be trained and advised by Soviet officers.

Would that be the extent of Soviet involvement? Or would Moscow follow Washington's lead and become more fully engaged? That could mean the United States would find itself fighting Soviet soldiers in the field.

Other possibilities occurred. The United States might tire of fighting Cubans in Central America and attack Cuba directly. If that happened, Soviet installations on the island might be damaged. Soviet citizens might be killed. Could this country expect the Soviet Union to accept either without striking back? Two decades ago, during the Cuban missile crisis, the Soviet Union had challenged the United States by attempting to arm Cuba with nuclear weapons. A U.S. president had threatened to retaliate with nuclear war. Would such threats and challenges be renewed during the course of a U.S. war in Central America? Would the ending of such an exchange be a compromise, as it was in 1962?

Congress was not alone in its concern. Around the country, citizens were growing troubled about what was going on. Some turned to their senators and representatives for information. Members of Congress visiting their states and districts found themselves flooded with questions — and criticisms. They learned that although most of their constituents approved of the Grenada invasion, fewer than 40 percent supported overall U.S. policy in Latin America. Other people sought answers about Central America from their churches. The Catholic Church in particular, because of its long involvement with the Catholic countries of Latin America, became a means through which citizens could learn about what was happening there. When priests, nuns, and missionaries stationed in Latin nations came home on leave, they were in demand as speakers and lecturers. Catholic concern about events in Central America was also sparked by the murders — at that point still unpunished — of the four churchwomen in El Salvador in 1980.

Across the United States, worried people began getting together. Many joined organizations such as Common Cause, the Center for Defense Information, and Clergy and Laity Concerned, all of which questioned U.S. policy in Central America. Some groups conducted prayer meetings and vigils. Others organized demonstrations similar to the antiwar protests of the Vietnam era. Some worked at raising money to help fight poverty, illness, and hunger in Latin America. Members of a group called Tools for Peace, for example, conducted drives to collect basic farming equipment to be distributed among the peasants of Nicaragua.

Other men and women chose to express their concern by helping Central Americans to escape the violence in their own countries and find safe new homes in the United States. Churches have been most deeply involved in this "sanctuary movement." By the mid-1980s, the movement had been officially endorsed by the governing bodies of the American Baptist Churches, the American Lutheran Church, the Disciples of Christ, the Presbyterian Church (U.S.A.), the United Church of Christ, the United Methodist Church, and the American Friends Service Committee. Several Catholic churches, and a number of nuns and priests, have offered sanctuary as well. So have Jewish congregations and their rabbis. More than half a million refugees, most of them from Guatemala and El Salvador, have entered this country with assistance from the movement. Many remain hidden in homes and churches today.

The Reagan administration strongly condemned the sanctuary movement, and early in 1985, the U.S. Justice Department announced the arrests of nearly a hundred of its workers. Those arrested were charged with transporting and harboring illegal aliens. The Justice Department action, however, seemed more likely to fuel the movement than to end it. "We will continue to assert the church's right to administer sanctuary to helpless people whose lives hang in the balance every day," said one arrested minister, the Reverend John M. Fife, of Southside Presbyterian Church in Tucson, Arizona.

Besides clamping down on the sanctuary movement, the Reagan administration found other ways to try to undercut groups that opposed its Latin American policies. One way was to attempt to build public support for those policies by convincing the nation that the Western Hemisphere was truly in danger of falling to communism. In 1983, the president appointed a twelve-member commission to visit Central America and report to him about what he believed to be the communist threat there, and about what the United States might do to avert that threat.

The president named members of both of this country's major political parties — Democratic and Republican — to the board. Doing that, he hoped, would make it more likely that both Democrats and Republicans in Congress would accept its findings. As head of the commission, he appointed Dr. Henry A. Kissinger, a former secretary of state. Like Reagan, Kissinger is a Republican. The members of the Kissinger Commission left for Central America in the middle of October and spent six days there. Returning to the United States, they devoted the next two and a half months to writing their report.

That report, released in January, echoed the president's fears. The Soviets were threatening "a coup of major proportions" in Central America. The report continued, ominously, "The concerting of Soviet and Cuban power . . . is a direct threat to United States security interests ... The crisis there [is] a crisis for the United States."

The commission's report stressed the opinion that this country must go on providing supplies and weapons to anticommunists all over Central America. We should give "significantly increased" military aid to El Salvador, and double our military aid to the rest of Central America. If we did not, the guerrilla war would drag on and on, a seemingly endless stalemate. But stalemates only appear endless, the report warned. "In a guerrilla war, a stalemate is not the same as a balance of power. It is in the nature of such a war that the insurgency is winning if it is not losing, and the government is losing if it is not winning." In other words, the United States and its allies must win a total victory in Central America — or lose all.

Winning, of course, would be expensive. It might cost the country as much as $12 billion by 1990. But if that money is not spent, "a sudden collapse [of anticommunist governments] is not inconceivable."

President Reagan was pleased by the commission's work, but to his critics, the report seemed less than convincing. One Latin expert, a former U.S. ambassador to the Dominican Republic named John Bartlow Martin, questioned the group's research methods. Its members "carried out their mission to six Central American countries in six days — or was it seven?" Martin asked sarcastically in a column in the *New York Times*. "I may be permitted to say that this is a lot of nonsense."

Martin pointed out that in 1961, he had been asked by President Kennedy to investigate conditions in the Dominican Republic after the overthrow of dictator Rafael Trujillo. Martin spent nineteen days in that one nation. "How can [Kissinger] possibly find out what's going on in six countries in six days?" he demanded. Perhaps, he suggested, it was because the commissioners spent almost no time talking with any leftists or ordinary citizens. Instead of trying to find out what was going on in Central America, and what people there thought about it, Kissinger and his fellow panelists relied upon information from government leaders — many of whom depended on U.S. aid to stay in power.

In Congress, too, many greeted the report with skepticism. They knew that some on the commission had disagreed privately with several of its conclusions. The disagreements had concerned such matters as whether or not the United States should insist upon an end to death squad activity in El Salvador, how much leeway the president should have in directing the military build-up in Central America, and whether the CIA's covert war ought to continue. Although the panel's few dissenters lost the arguments — Kissinger insisted that anticommunism was more important than other considerations — many in Congress agreed with them. Money was another problem on the minds of senators and representatives. Twelve billion dollars by 1990? "No way," an aide to one member of Congress declared.

Not long after the Kissinger report was made public, a new debate arose. In April 1984, the world learned about the CIA mining of Nicaraguan harbors. Not only had six Nicaraguan ships been damaged, so had six vessels belonging to five other nations. Ten sailors had been seriously injured.

The world reacted indignantly. "An act of piracy," cried the Soviet Union, one of whose tankers was struck. "Very dangerous to international traffic on the high seas," said British Prime Minister Margaret Thatcher. Usually an enthusiastic backer of Reagan's policies, Thatcher opposed the mining. So did the government of another U.S. ally, France.

Nicaragua's response to the mining was to appeal to the World Court. This court was established in 1945 as part of the United Nations. Its fifteen judges, from nations around the world, sit at The Hague, in the Netherlands. Their job is to settle legal disputes between countries, although they have no power to enforce their decisions. Nevertheless, nations, including the United States, generally abide by World Court decisions. Only if a decision has to do with internal matters will the United States refuse to honor it.

And that was just what the harbor mining was,

White House spokespersons maintained. It was an internal matter involving the rights and responsibilities of the CIA. The World Court had no jurisdiction over that agency and the United States would pay no attention to any ruling that concerned it.

The court went ahead anyway. On May 10, its judges declared that the mining was illegal under international law. By a vote of 15–0, the court ordered the United States to stop it. Further World Court proceedings were scheduled for 1985. In January of that year, however, the United States announced that it was walking out on the case. This was the first time this country had ever done such a thing.

The mining operation also caused an uproar at home. Members of Congress, both Democrats and Republicans, were furious when they discovered what had been going on. "I think it's wrong, wrong, wrong," said Clarence D. Long, a Democratic representative from Maryland. Thomas P. O'Neill, Jr., Democrat of Massachusetts and Speaker of the House of Representatives, thought the same. "I have contended that the Reagan administration's secret war against Nicaragua was morally indefensible," the Speaker reminded the House. "Today it is clear that it is legally indefensible as well."

Republican Senator Barry Goldwater of Arizona felt the same way. Goldwater is a conservative, and a long-time crusader against communism, but he could not condone the mining as a method of fighting against communism. Nor did he like the fact that no one in Congress had been informed about the operation.

"The president has asked us to back his foreign policy," Senator Goldwater wrote angrily to CIA Director William Casey. "Bill, how can we back his foreign policy when we don't know what the hell he is doing? . . . Mine the harbors of Nicaragua? This is an act violating international law. It is an act of war. For the life of me, I don't see how we are going to explain it."

On April 10, the United States Senate voted to condemn the mining. The vote was 84–12, with forty-two of the Senate's fifty-four Republicans joining in the majority. A day later, the House also expressed its disapproval of the CIA action. Although the congressional votes were not legally binding upon the president, they served their purpose. A month before the World Court issued its 1984 ruling, the White House announced that the mining would not continue.

The covert war itself, however, would. The Reagan administration stuck to its position: The Sandinistas were supplying El Salvador's leftists, thus giving them the means to go on fighting. Therefore the United States must continue harassing Nicaragua. The only purpose of the CIA secret war was to force the Sandinistas to give up their effort to export revolution, administration officials repeated.

Actually, that was not the real purpose at all, responded one former member of the CIA, David C. MacMichael. Until July 1983, MacMichael had been a CIA analyst, whose assignment was to study and report on Sandinista involvement in the fighting in El Salvador.

"The whole picture that the administration has presented of Salvadoran insurgent operations being planned, directed, and supplied from Nicaragua is simply not true," he told reporters ten months after leaving the CIA. "There has not been a successful interdiction, or a verified report, of arms moving from Nicaragua to El Salvador since April 1981."

If MacMichael was right, the Sandinistas were not supplying the rebels — and the CIA knew it. Why would CIA officials then insist that they were? MacMichael offered his opinion. "The administration and the CIA have systematically misrepresented Nicaraguan involvement in the supply of arms to Salvadoran guerrillas to justify its efforts to overthrow the Nicaraguan government."

MacMichael's charge created a fresh debate. Was the United States once more trying to unseat an unfriendly Latin American government and replace it with a pro–United States regime? Many thought so.

But others denied it, and they denied the truth of MacMichael's accusation as well. A few months after the former agent went public with his charges, the administration gave its side of the story. Speaking for the administration was General Paul C. Gorman, then head of the Southern Command in Panama.

At a news conference in August, General Gorman told reporters that Salvadoran army units had captured weapons being smuggled into the country by boat. They had also seized maps of Sandinista supply routes. The general displayed photos and television tapes that he said showed crates of guns being moved from "mother ships" into small canoes. The films and pictures were blurry and indistinct, wrote a *New York Times* reporter, Charles Mohr. With one exception, they were too difficult to make out. That one exception did, according to Mohr, appear to show a crate being unloaded from a canoe.

To MacMichael, however, such evidence was of doubtful value. "Within the CIA," he said, "there is pressure to bend information to fit policy." Within months, that charge was repeated by another former CIA agent, John R. Horton. Horton resigned from the agency in 1984, after he says he was ordered to write reports that falsely exaggerated left-wing activity in Mexico. Within the agency, Horton said then, "There is pressure to jigger estimates to conform with policy."

Horton's testimony lent weight to MacMichael's. If his story was true, people thought, the CIA might well be "jiggering estimates" about Nicaraguan arms shipments, too. The accounts of the two former agents became one more reason for congressional reluctance to approve Reagan's requests for additional money to finance covert actions against the Sandinistas.

Already, by early 1984, funds for that purpose were running out. Yet the war continued. Where was the money coming from?

Evidence gathered from government documents showed that the Department of Defense (DOD) had been supplying it. DOD officials had been selling ships, planes, guns, and other equipment to the CIA at prices far below their actual value. Department officials had also spent $200,000 to modernize a Honduran air base. Then they gave the base to the CIA. They had provided millions of dollars' worth of training to Honduran soldiers, built two radar stations in Central America, and supplied high-speed boats for arms interdiction.

The record also showed why the DOD could afford to be so generous. In some cases, money appropriated by Congress for one purpose was used for something quite different. In others, funds were secretly transferred from one account to another. The radar stations, for instance, were paid for with money that Congress intended to go toward routine maintenance.

Behind-the-scenes financing for CIA operations also came through private organizations. As we saw in the preceding chapter, administration officials estimated that such groups were supplying Central

America's anticommunists at the rate of about $1.5 million a month in 1984. The officials compared such aid to the Central American aid being provided by groups like Tools for Peace.

To many, however, the comparison did not seem apt. Tools for Peace really was a private organization, they protested. It had no ties to government. By contrast, the organizations supporting *contra* activity were doing so with cooperation from the White House, the State Department, and the DOD. The goods they supplied were deliberately used to thwart Congress's efforts to reduce covert activity in Central America. The Reagan administration was willing to "push the law to its limits" to pay for its Central American policies, Representative Lee Hamilton complained. Other congressional critics of the way the United States was funding its secret war included Thomas P. O'Neill, Jr., of Massachusetts and Representative Jim Wright of Texas.

Congressional irritation over clandestine funding of a clandestine war was bad news for President Reagan. But bad news was balanced by good. On May 6, 1984, José Napoleón Duarte was elected president of El Salvador. A month later he was inaugurated, pledging to lead his country toward democracy.

Duarte was generally regarded as an honest man with genuine democratic ideals. Most members of Congress, even those most critical of Reagan's Latin policies, thought Duarte would do his best to control El Salvador's military, to end death squad activity, and to promote social justice and land reform. Yet despite their faith in Duarte's personal integrity, many in Congress wondered about democracy's future in El Salvador. Their doubts began with the election. Had it really been as free and fair as U.S. officials claimed?

The doubts centered around U.S. involvement in the election process. This country had acted as a sort of unofficial overseer through out the campaign. When Salvadoran election officials complained that counting the votes made them tired, for example, the U.S. ambassador to El Salvador, Thomas Pickering, chided them. Tallying the results was more important than their beauty sleep, he said. Would we in the United States feel we had enjoyed a free and fair election with some foreign diplomat keeping an eye on the proceedings and making gentle jokes at our expense?

How would we feel if the government of another country helped pay the campaign expenses of one of our presidential candidates? That is what the United States did in El Salvador. Officially, Duarte received $2 million from the United States. It may have been more. Many suspected that additional funds were secretly funneled into his campaign through the CIA. But assume it was only the $2 million. Since El Salvador has a population of 5 million, that amounts to a contribution of 40 cents per person. In the United States, with its population of over 226 million, a foreign campaign contribution of 40 cents per person would come to more than $90 million.

One senator was furious at what he considered a blatant attempt by this country to manage the Salvadoran election. Ambassador Pickering had used his influence to "strangle liberty in the night," said Jesse Helms, Republican of North Carolina. Helms, an extreme conservative, backed the candidacy of Salvadoran politician Roberto d'Aubuisson, a radical right-winger.

As the months passed, doubts about the election became concern about Duarte's ability to bring democracy to a land that had never known it. Could he really control the death squads? It was true that five low-ranking Salvadoran soldiers had gone to jail for the 1980 murders of four U.S. churchwomen. But what about the officers who had ordered or permitted the killings? What about those who had condoned them afterward? What about those who had helped cover up the crime for four years? Who were they? Was Duarte going to see to it that they went on trial too?

Even Duarte's most enthusiastic backers had to admit it was unlikely. According to a 1984 U.S. State Department investigation, one of those responsible for organizing and running the squads was a man named Eugenio Vides Casanova. Casanova was the minister of defense in Duarte's government. Other leading politicians mentioned in connection with death squads included Roberto d'Aubuisson and Colonel Nicolas Carranza. Carranza was head of the country's Treasury Police under Duarte.

If a U.S. president learned that two of the most important members of his administration might be guilty of heinous crimes, he could simply ask them to step down from office. They could be charged and put on trial. In El Salvador, it's not so easy. The military has always had power over civilian politicians there. If Duarte did try to remove Carranza and Casanova from office, he might well face a death squad himself some dark night. Salvadoran death squads do not limit their attacks to the weak and helpless. In March 1980, the country's Roman Catholic archbishop, Oscar Arnulfo Romero, was murdered by members of one squad as he said Mass in a chapel in San Salvador.

Unable to get the death squads under quick control, Duarte — and the United States — had to watch as killings actually increased after the May 1984 election. In July, sixty-eight unarmed peasants were slain by officers and soldiers in eight small villages near Los Llanitos in the central part of the country. Two months later, thirty-four died in another massacre.

Land reform, too, presented a problem. El Salvador's reform program had gotten under way in 1980.

Haciendas, some of which had belonged to the same families for generations, were broken up. Some land went to individuals; some was turned over to groups of people to manage and cultivate together. One sugar cane cutter, who, like his father and grandfather before him, had been born on a rich man's estate, tried to describe how it felt to be a landowner. "How can I tell you what this meant to me?" he asked. "My family and I were *colonos,* farm laborers who were treated like animals . . . I was now in an office."

Two years later, administration of the land reform program was handed over to the political party headed by Roberto d'Aubuisson. As an ultraconservative, d'Aubuisson was devoted to maintaining the ancient feudal rights of the wealthy landed class. He and his followers began dismantling the land reform program. At the same time, attacks by army units and death squads made it more and more difficult for peasants to operate their new farms. Land reform faltered.

On June 28, 1984, it died. Less than a month after Duarte took office, El Salvador's Legislative Assembly — the nation's lawmaking body — voted to end the most important remaining part of the program. "We were, once again, *colonos,*" lamented the cane cutter, his optimism of four years earlier destroyed.

Land reform seemed to be over. Death squad activity was continuing. The Salvadoran military was still not under civilian control. All this bothered many in Congress and around the country. Equally troubling, many felt, was the apparent willingness of the Reagan administration to ignore the facts. Two headlines on the same page of the September 15, 1984, *New York Times* told the story: SALVADORAN VILLAGERS REPORT ATTACK BY ARMY, said the first, referring to the July and September massacres of civilians. Directly below this article was another headline: SHULTZ CERTIFIES THAT SALVADORANS ARE ELIGIBLE FOR MORE MILITARY AID.

Public disquietude was stirred afresh the next month. This time the issue was a small blue booklet, *Psychological Operations in Guerrilla Warfare*. The volume, prepared by the CIA for use by Nicaraguan *contras,* was a how-to manual for terrorists.

In forty-four Spanish-language pages, *Psychological Operations in Guerrilla Warfare* offered precise instruction on ways the *contras* might turn mob violence to their benefit. With words and drawings, it told how to infiltrate towns and cities in order to inflict damage on Sandinista facilities. It listed methods for getting ordinary citizens to work against the government. Blackmail them into doing it, was one suggestion. The manual also covered the subject of "neutralization" of government officials. "Neutralization" is a common CIA euphemism for "assassination."

The little book created yet another controversy in

Washington. Even the most senior members of the House and Senate had known nothing of it. If they had, they might have been surprised. Since 1976, CIA officials have been absolutely forbidden to have anything to do with promoting assassination.

"The manual is a disaster for United States foreign policy," declared Representative Edward Boland of Massachusetts. "I am appalled by the image of the United States that the primer portrays."

So was Senator Claiborne Pell of Rhode Island. "We seem to be engaged in the very same terrorist activities which we deplore elsewhere," he said.

Senator Christopher J. Dodd of Connecticut concurred. "This administration has been vociferous in its condemnation of state-supported terrorism," he pointed out. "This document makes a mockery of that position. If this isn't state-supported terrorism, then I don't know what is."

That was what bothered so many, in Congress and around the nation. How could the United States criticize Nicaragua, Cuba, and the Soviet Union for exporting revolution and indulging in terrorism and then turn around and employ the very same tactics itself? Can it be morally right to fight terror with terror? people were asking themselves. Can it even be good policy?

8

Old Assumptions or
New Ideas?

By the mid-1980s, the debate over U.S. policy in Latin America involved a great many specific questions. How much should Congress vote to spend in El Salvador? Should the CIA's covert war continue? Should the United States go on funding the anti-Sandinista *contras?* Was the Reagan administration preparing for a major war? Underlying all the specific questions, however, were more fundamental ones. They concerned the basic assumptions behind past and present policy in Latin America.

One assumption is that Latin rebellion and insurrection must always be inspired from outside. Back in the early days of U.S.–Latin American relations, the outsiders were assumed to be European imperialists. Today they are assumed to be communist agents from the Soviet Union, Cuba, or Nicaragua. But both then and now, the unrest has been seen as foreign. That — according to the Monroe Doctrine — makes it a U.S. responsibility to deal with.

Another assumption is that military solutions

work best in Latin America. Nearly all U.S. presidents have believed this. President Ronald Reagan did, when he and his advisers mapped out their Central American strategy. Communism, the president was convinced, can be defeated on the battlefield. Once its defenders are dead, or thoroughly weakened and intimidated, there will be an end to leftist activity.

Are such assumptions valid? Some doubt it. To them, it seems unlikely that leftist unrest in Latin America is simply the work of foreign agents. Not that such agents do not exist. Beyond doubt, there have been Soviets in Cuba, Cubans in Nicaragua and Grenada, and so on. The Soviets and Cubans have shown themselves eager to turn unrest to their advantage.

But have they created the unrest in the first place? Critics of U.S. policy do not believe so. Latin unrest, they are convinced, owes more to the area's tremendous social, economic, and political problems than it does to outside agitators.

If that is the case, military might alone is not going to end the unrest and keep communism out of Latin America. In fact, the critics add, militarism is just one more Latin problem, a problem that makes all the other problems worse. And the worse those problems get, the more likely it is that Latin Americans will develop communist sympathies. U.S. policy in Latin America, they conclude, may be doing as much to propel the area toward communism as it is to prevent its spread.

Are they right? If so, the propulsion continues. In June 1985, Congress voted to allow President Reagan to spend more millions of dollars to support the Nicaraguan *contras* in their fight against the Sandinista government. At the same time, the nation's lawmakers agreed to permit the president to order new U.S. covert military action aimed at undermining that government. "A declaration of war against Nicaragua" was the way Representative Bill Alexander of Arkansas described the vote. Speaker of the House O'Neill was even more blunt. "He [Reagan] is not going to be happy until he has our Marines and our Rangers in there with a complete victory," the Speaker warned.

Millions of people around the country shared these men's distress. A poll taken by the *New York Times* and CBS News just days before the vote in Congress showed that more than half the population flatly opposed U.S. military involvement — open or secret — in Nicaragua. Two-thirds favored sending food and medicines to the *contras,* but fewer than a quarter were willing to provide them with military aid. Unlike a majority of their elected leaders, the people of the United States were coming to feel that it is time for this country to abandon its old approaches to Latin America. We need to fashion *new* policies for the area, they believe, policies that are based on fresh assumptions and firmly grounded in the realities of Latin life.

The first reality is poverty. This is a reality inherited from the days of the Iberian monarchs and their *conquistadores*. It is a reality perpetuated over the years by the *hacienda* system, and by the slavery, *encomienda*, and debt peonage that supported that system. It is a reality carried into the present in part by the continued unequal distribution of land and wealth in most of Latin America.

At the beginning of the 1970s in Peru, 0.4 percent of the population — less than half of one percent — owned three-quarters of the farmable land. When the Sandinistas seized power in Nicaragua in 1979, 2 percent of the country's people held nearly 80 percent of the land. Landownership figures in Guatemala and El Salvador were approximately the same. That meant that a small percentage of Latin Americans enjoyed great wealth. For nearly all the rest, poverty was a fact of everyday life.

In Mexico, the minimum daily wage is $4.41. (All money figures are in U.S. equivalents.) In Haiti, the poorest nation in the hemisphere, the average income per person is $280 a year. In El Salvador, it is $470. In Brazil, a farm laborer may earn $80 a month. For that, he works six ten-hour days a week on a *fazenda* — a huge estate.

Wages like these doom millions of Latin Americans to a miserable life. In Brazil's largest cities, such as São Paulo and Rio de Janeiro, one-sixth of the population lives in *favelas* — great sprawling slums that ring the shining skyscrapers and flower-filled plazas where the city's well-to-do work and play. "Houses" in the *favelas* are constructed of rags, scraps of wood, cardboard, bits of sheet metal. There is no garbage collection; there are no showers, no toilets. A single cold-water faucet may serve thousands. Such slums exist throughout Latin America: *callampas* (mushrooms) in Chile; *barrios suburbanos* (suburbs) in Equador; *pueblos jovens* (new towns) in Peru.

Conditions in the slums make for an abysmal public health record. In Colombia, life expectancy for men is sixty-five years. In Bolivia, it is sixty-one; in Honduras, fifty-three. Each year in Mexico City, air pollution kills nearly a hundred thousand people, one-third of them children. Contaminated water is another problem there. So is a lack of health care. Says one Mexican politician, "We calculate that fifty percent of the Mexico City population has no access to medical treatment." Of every 1000 babies born in Brazil, 92 will die before a year is up. In the country's most destitute communities, the rate soars to 250 deaths per 1000 births. Half the young men who offer themselves for service in Brazil's military must be turned down. They were so poorly nourished as children that they will never be fit for army life.

Brazilian children also have an excellent chance of

being abandoned by parents too poor to care for them. Officials are not sure exactly how many homeless girls and boys roam the *favelas*. Perhaps it is fifteen million, perhaps twenty. All are age fifteen or less. Although the abandoned-children problem is worst in Brazil, it exists all over Latin America. Many of the abandoned turn to crime to feed themselves. So do thousands of others whose need is almost as great. Since the police seem unable to control crime or to catch the criminals, citizens may take the law into their own hands. In Brazil, lynchings are becoming common. One day in 1983, a middle-aged São Paulo man chased and caught a fifteen-year-old robber. In front of witnesses, he threw the boy to the ground and stomped on him until he was dead. No charges were brought against the man.

Not only do the great majority of individual Latins live in poverty, their countries are poor, too. During the 1970s, most Latin nations undertook numerous large construction projects. Broad highways began cutting through tropical rain forests. Tall bridges spanned remote rivers and deep mountain chasms. Electrical power stations and modern office buildings sprang up. At the same time, most Latin nations were spending millions on military and riot control equipment, tanks, guns, and ammunition. Latin America was entering the late twentieth century — on borrowed money. Unable to finance the building projects and the military build-ups on their own, Latin nations borrowed from banks around the world. By the 1980s, they were deeply in debt.

In debt and without the means to repay what they owed. Some nations were unable to pay even the interest on their loans. In 1985, Mexico's debt amounted to $93 billion. Brazil's was $98 billion. Two other countries in deep trouble, Argentina and Venezuela, owed $45 billion and $35 billion, respectively. Latin America's debt problem had become a crisis.

Afraid that they might never get their money back, international bankers began, in 1984, to make arrangements to allow Latin governments to repay their debts more slowly than usual. They, and the debtor nations, had hopes that the arrangements would work out. But already, much damage had been done. Latin American economies were in a mess. Unemployment was high. So were prices.

Unemployment and price inflation were related to the debt. Much of the borrowed money had gone for construction projects, many of which had to be abandoned, unfinished, as the money ran out. Latin leaders might have been wiser to have spent the funds on setting up new factories or on improving farmland. Farms and factories offer lasting jobs. Construction projects do not, and neither does spending for military purposes. By 1984, Argentine unemployment stood at 17 percent. In the Dominican Republic, it was 40 percent, and in Guatemala, 50 percent.

Added to unemployment is the problem of "underemployment." Underemployed people are those who have been forced to settle for jobs unsuited to their training and abilities. The underemployed of Latin America include university graduates as well as skilled workers.

Rising prices were also tied to the debt crisis. Money became scarcer as nations struggled to repay their loans. Manufactured goods were in short supply, thanks to the lack of plants and factories. Before long, the combined scarcities were driving prices up at a terrifying rate. In 1984, inflation in Mexico was running at 161 percent; in Brazil, it was 170 percent; in Nicaragua, 300 percent. In Argentina and Bolivia, it was 1000 percent. That meant that something that cost one U.S. dollar in January cost $11 the next December.

People who face an inflation rate of 1000 percent may feel desperate. So may those who cannot find work no matter how hard they look, or those who feel they must administer their own justice or do without. Desperation comes easily to abandoned children and to parents forced to desert them. It must be a permanent state of mind for men and women who know that they will never live anywhere but in a Brazilian *favela* or a Chilean *callampa*. Anything must seem better than such a fate. Communism, for instance.

Communism promises that it will take from the rich and give to the poor. Castro in Cuba, Allende in Chile, the Sandinistas in Nicaragua — all acted promptly to take over the *haciendas* of the wealthy and turn the land over to the needy. Not directly to the needy, to be sure. In a communist state, the means of production — farms, factories, mines, and the like — are held by the state in the name of the people. The farms are cultivated, the factories kept humming, the mines worked, by men and women who toil for the state, not for themselves. Profits go to the government, rather than to themselves as individuals. They are paid, by the government, for their labor.

To United States citizens, this may seem an unsatisfactory system. People should not have to work for the state, they believe. They should be able to work for themselves, to benefit from the fruits of their labor. Everyone should have the right to start a business. Workers are entitled to keep their profits.

In the United States, this argument makes sense. This is a rich nation, with a large middle class. Members of that middle class may work for someone else, but if they want to, they can usually find the means and the money to start their own businesses. Some may become rich themselves. But what about Latin America?

There, the anticommunist argument loses some of its force. Latin America has a tiny rich upper class and a huge poverty-ridden lower one. It has a relatively small middle class. Few Latins — except those who are rich to begin with — will ever be able to start a business or to pile up profits. Great numbers of them can't even find work. Economically, the present system in Latin America seems to offer little to the bulk of the people.

Communism may seem to offer more. So what, Latin Americans might say, if we still won't own our own farms or businesses under communism? At least we will get — through our government — to share in them, and to share in their profits. Perhaps that is not much, compared to what people in the United States are accustomed to. But it is more than most of us have today. It is more than most of us have had for the past five hundred years.

Any U.S. policy that overlooks the fact that communism may seem to offer something positive to the desperate of Latin America is sure to fail in the end, critics of present policy warn. U.S. leaders must recognize that, much as they themselves dislike communism, people in the *favelas* may have reason to feel differently.

That does not mean that the United States ought to stand aside and watch Latin America rush to embrace communism. It doesn't mean that most Latin Americans, even the poorest, want to embrace it. It does mean that many in Latin America may be desperate enough to embrace communism even though they do not especially like it.

A wise policy would take that into account, the critics maintain. It would recognize Latin desperation and reach out to help. If this country wants to stop communism permanently in Latin America, it must do all it can to eliminate the social and economic problems that help give communism its appeal.

This country's leaders could promote land reform more actively, for example. They might offer economic "rewards" — gifts and low-interest loans — to nations that adopt reform programs. They could offer more economic aid to enable Latin nations to improve health care, to construct decent housing, to feed their children.

But what does the United States do instead? the critics demand. In 1961, President Kennedy asked Congress for money for an Alliance for Progress. The money was not forthcoming, and Latin poverty deepened. Twenty years later, the Reagan administration actually opposed land reform in El Salvador. Only when Congress made it clear that without reform there would be no military aid to the Salvadoran government, did the president agree to go along with it. Later, his secretary of state told Congress that the redistribution program was going nicely when, in fact, it had been discontinued.

In Sandinista Nicaragua, on the other hand, Latin American peasants could see land reform moving ahead, even if it was being carried out along communist lines. Nicaraguans also know that under the Sandinistas, 340 health centers were built within five years. According to United States citizens who visited Nicaragua, malnutrition in children there was down by nearly 75 percent since the Sandinista victory. Diseases like polio, diphtheria, and measles had been all but eliminated. Infant mortality dropped 25 percent between 1978 and 1982.

Nicaragua still had a long way to go. Life expectancy for males was only fifty-one years in the early 1980s. Nevertheless, people there had reason to feel that the Sandinistas had done more for them in five years than the Somozas had in forty. Communism is far from being an ideal system, they may say. But can a job on a state-run farm be worse than starvation in a slum?

A second reality that the United States needs to consider is Latin political history and tradition. That tradition is not democratic but authoritarian. It is not liberal but repressive. It does not include open elections and representative government but rigged votes and dictatorial powers. And it has been that way since Christopher Columbus founded the first New World colony in 1493. It was that way through three hundred years of Spanish and Portuguese rule and, with rare exceptions, through the era of the nineteenth-century *caudillos.* It remains that way today in much of Latin America.

It was that way in Sandinista Nicaragua, as President Reagan often pointed out. Under communist rule, the Nicaraguan press was censored. In 1983, 540 opponents of the government were in jail. Since the communist takeover in 1979, 90 Nicaraguans had been murdered by death squads. The country's 1984 election was, in Reagan's words, a "phony" and a "sham." Leaders of three of the nation's eight opposition political parties refused to take part in it. Campaigning and voting procedures were sure to be dishonest, they said, and they wanted no part of them. Although five other opposition groups were scheduled to appear on the ballot with the Sandinistas, it was a foregone conclusion that the Sandinista candidate for president, Daniel Ortega, would win.

The opposition leaders were right. Despite the other names on the ballot, Ortega did win. The election went smoothly, with exactly the result the Sandinistas had planned for.

But how did that election compare to Nicaraguan elections in the Somoza days? The Somozas had seized and held power through a series of coups and dishonest votes. So what had Nicaraguans lost by turning to communism? Certainly not the freedom of the ballot box.

Nicaraguans knew the United States had helped

place the Somozas in power in their country. In 1984, many also suspected that the United States was also responsible, at least in part, for the failure of the three opposition leaders to participate in their election. These opposition activists claimed, days before the voting, that U.S. officials in Nicaragua had urged them to stay out of the race.

Why? One U.S. official, speaking anonymously, gave an answer. "The administration never contemplated letting Cruz [Arturo José Cruz, one of the opposition leaders] stay in the race, because then the Sandinistas could justifiably claim that the elections were legitimate, making it much harder for the United States to oppose the Nicaraguan government," the official said. Commenting on this, John B. Oakes, former editor of the *New York Times,* wrote, "The most fraudulent thing about the Nicaraguan election was the part the Reagan administration played in it."

Critics also questioned Reagan's assertion that the Sandinistas had worsened political conditions in Nicaragua and made it a "totalitarian dungeon." Of course the Sandinista government was no model of democracy. But how did it stack up against the Somoza regime? Was it any worse? Was it better in some ways? And how did the Sandinista government compare to noncommunist, or anticommunist, governments elsewhere in Latin America? the critics asked.

Consider Chile. As Nicaraguans went to the polls in November 1984, Chileans were wishing they could go too. By then, they were well into their second decade of life under an anticommunist military dictatorship.

"We have gone through some very difficult years," a Chilean priest said then, "confronting killings, tortures, concentration camps, and atrocities of all kinds." One politician in the country described the government of dictator Augusto Pinochet Ugarte as "the worst government in the history of Chile." Like Nicaragua under both the Sandinistas and the Somozas, Chile had no free press. Its 1978 election, which Pinochet "won," was considered fraudulent. Pressed by an angry public to call for new elections in 1984, the general stepped up his repressive tactics. He refused to schedule a vote. "There will be no elections," he stated. "I don't have confidence in orthodox democracy."

That was a sentiment Pinochet apparently shared with other Latin leaders. In elections scheduled for November 1984 in Uruguay, one man who announced his intention of becoming a candidate was Wilson Ferriera Aldunate. A popular man with democratic views, Aldunate had spent several years in exile. Returning to Uruguay with his son to take part in the campaign, Aldunate was thrown into prison. So was his son. Although the Uruguayan election was held, the name Aldunate was not listed on the ballot.

As a matter of fact, a number of Latin American heads of government were not believers in orthodox democracy — nor in any other kind of democracy — as 1985 began. Military officers held power, directly or indirectly, in El Salvador, Panama, Guatemala, and Honduras. They ruled in Paraguay and Chile. In other countries, Haiti, for example, rule was by civilian dictatorship.

Even Latin countries that observe democratic forms may not be democracies in the sense that the United States is. The 1984 election in Uruguay, as we saw, was held without the participation of the leading candidate. The 1985 election that replaced Brazil's military regime with a civilian government was not a popular one. No ordinary Brazilian citizens were permitted to vote; only a few score of the nation's top politicians had the opportunity to cast a ballot.

In Mexico, political opposition is allowed, and elections are open. Yet a single party — the Institutional Revolutionary Party — has won every presidential election since 1929. It has won every governorship race, too, and most local contests. The party's political opponents agree that many of these victories have been the result of election fraud. Mexico's Institutional Revolutionary Party controls lawmaking and politics throughout the nation. Its head, the president of Mexico, appoints officials to run every town and city from the Rio Grande to the Guatemalan border. In addition, the party manages 75 percent of the Mexican economy.

Peru is another nation with an elected president and many of the institutions of democracy. Yet brutality and repression lie just beneath the surface there. Police and army death squads roam the countryside, raping, murdering, torturing. In 1983 alone, they were responsible for at least twenty-seven hundred killings, according to human rights groups. Compared to that, ninety Sandinista death squad killings in four years does not seem quite so many. Compared to forty thousand government and army killings in El Salvador between 1979 and 1984, ninety *turba* murders pale.

Compared to the lack of democracy — the kind of democracy we in the United States are used to — in other parts of Latin America, the democratic deficiencies of Nicaragua may also seem less significant. Yet the United States condemns those deficiencies, while supporting — or at any rate not criticizing — other nations where conditions are as bad, or worse. The reason for this, many believe, is that U.S. policy tends to confuse anticommunism with democracy in Latin America.

Communism is an economic system; democracy, a political one. A communist nation may be undemocratic. The Soviet Union is an example of one that is both. But just because a country is not communist does not mean that it is automatically a democracy. Latin America is full of examples of noncommunist nations that are undemocratic in the extreme.

Many Latins fear it will be even fuller of them if the United States has its way. The CIA-backed *contra* force in Nicaragua was dominated by former members of Anastasio Somoza's National Guard in 1984. Few believed that the Guardsmen had much interest in democracy. They were fighting for a return to conservative dictatorship and to the dishonest elections, censorship, and right-wing police and army terror that distinguish such dictatorships. Yet President Reagan referred to these Guardsmen as "freedom fighters," and urged Congress to vote more and more millions for them. Simultaneously, the United States was cutting itself off from those liberal *contras* who broke with the Sandinista government over its failure to practice democracy. What will Nicaragua be like if the right-wing *contras* do win?

What will El Salvador be like if its government wins its battle to defeat the country's leftist rebels? Even with the U.S. Congress monitoring events there, U.S. policy was emphasizing anticommunism at the expense of human rights. A government victory and a withdrawal of U.S. observers might well signal a swing back to authoritarian government acting for the sole benefit of the rich and powerful.

Of course, the U.S. policy of favoring stability and conservatism over democracy and human rights in Latin America was nothing new in the 1980s. Such a policy goes back to the beginning, to the early years of the Monroe Doctrine and U.S. support for the *caudillos* of the 1800s. It was in place through the years of dollar diplomacy and gunboat diplomacy, through the construction of the Panama Canal and the decades of the Platt Amendment, through military occupations in the Dominican Republic, Haiti, Nicaragua, and other nations.

If such a policy continues into the future, Latin Americans will find it difficult to change much. Efforts toward land redistribution and social reform will falter, and most of the population will remain poverty-stricken, trapped in a semifeudal way of life. Democracy cannot flourish under such conditions, and violence, tyranny, and militarism will continue to mark Latin political life.

Militarism, tyranny, violence, and poverty — these are the very conditions out of which, many believe, much left-wing unrest is born. Can the United States commit itself to helping to prolong such conditions and still keep Latin America free of spreading communism? If not, and if the United States refuses to alter its old policies and its old assumptions, what hope can there be for Latin America?

9

The Future of Latin America: Final Battlefield or Finally Free?

On October 15, 1984, a historic meeting took place in the town of La Palma in northern El Salvador. The meeting was between President Duarte and one of the nation's top leftist guerrilla leaders, Fermán Cienfuegos. The two discussed El Salvador's civil war and what might be done to end it.

Duarte proposed that the rebels agree to participate in elections for El Salvador's National Assembly scheduled to be held in March 1985. Leftists who won seats in the assembly would be free to take them, he said. Cienfuegos said his followers would be willing to take part in the voting *if* Duarte would also consent to offer some of them a share in the Salvadoran government even *before* March. To this, Duarte would not agree. The men parted in a friendly manner, however, and agreed to meet again.

Was the meeting a step toward bringing peace to El Salvador? Or was it an empty and meaningless gesture?

As far as the United States was concerned, it was

the latter. Officials at the United States embassy in San Salvador made clear their feeling that Duarte and the leftists had nothing to discuss — except the terms of a leftist surrender. The Reagan administration was standing by its assumption that military solutions are best in Latin America. In the month after the La Palma meeting, this country undertook a new series of military maneuvers in the Caribbean similar to, although not as extensive as, Big Pine II. U.S. President Reagan, re-elected in November 1984, again asked Congress to increase military aid to Central America's anticommunists. Guns and troops — they had won the day in Grenada, and they would do the same in the rest of Latin America, the president remained convinced. Discussions in small Salvadoran towns would accomplish nothing.

Many in Latin America thought otherwise, however, and they regarded La Palma in a different light. More than anyone else, Latins are aware of the effect that five centuries of militarism have had upon their land and their people. Weary of the violence, millions of Latins saw the 1980s as the time to begin taking a new approach.

Among them was Belisario Betancur Cuartas, president of Colombia. Colombia is one of Latin America's strongest democracies. In 1983, Betancur visited New York City to address a meeting of the UN General Assembly. His speech was an eloquent appeal to the world's two superpowers — the United

States and the Soviet Union — to withdraw their arms and their advisers from Latin America and to leave its nations to work out their own problems.

"Whoever the arms suppliers are," Betancur said, "they should leave. The Central American nations alone must find an answer."

To find that answer, Betancur has employed more than eloquence. For eighteen months during 1983 and 1984, he applied himself to working out agreements to end more than twenty-five years of left-wing rebel activity in Colombia. The agreements, between Betancur's government and the leaders of three major leftist groups, were signed in March and August of 1984.

Under the "pacts of honor," Colombian leftists promised to cease their guerrilla warfare for an indefinite period of time. "There will not be one shot more," said one rebel leader. During the peace, the Colombian government pledged to pursue a "radical" land reform program. It would write new laws to make it easier for members of left-wing groups to run for and win political office. Its officials would continue to talk to and negotiate with the leftists. This would be the beginning of a "national dialogue," Betancur and the rebels agreed.

There were those, in both Colombia and the United States, who expressed skepticism about the pacts. Some rebels had refused to sign them. Some who did set a date, May 28, 1985, as the last day of the cease-fire. That deadline might be extended, but it also might not. One way or another, fighting in Colombia was sure to continue, many believed.

Other criticisms were heard. Colombia conservatives complained that the agreements were ill-advised "rewards" for terrorism. Rather than promise political and social reforms, they said, Betancur should have promised continued persecution if the rebels did not give up their fight. But Betancur pointed out that more than three decades of military effort had failed to subdue the leftists. During the ten years between 1948 and 1958, two hundred thousand Colombians had died in the fighting. La Violencia, those dreadful years were called. It was time for the country to replace violence with political solutions, Betancur told his people.

It was time for other Latin nations to attempt the same, Betancur was convinced. In January 1983, he and other members of his government traveled to the lovely Panamanian resort island of Contadora. There, they met with representatives of three other countries, Mexico, Venezuela, and Panama. Together, they came up with a tentative peace plan — the Contadora plan — for Central America.

The Contadora proposal is for a twenty-point treaty. It calls for reductions in arms, troops, and foreign military advisers in all of Central America, and for prohibiting the construction of military bases by outsiders, communist or noncommunist. It asks for an end to the supplying of arms to antigovernment rebels by the United States and its allies, as well as by the Soviet Union and its communist friends. Finally, Contadora is a plan to bring democracy to Central America. It provides for fair laws and impartial courts, for the freeing of political prisoners, for free elections, and for guarantees of other civil and human rights.

From the outset, the United States government was unenthusiastic about Contadora. Although it gave official support to what the Contadora nations were doing, members of the Reagan administration did little to ensure the plan's acceptance. Despite U.S. coolness, however, Colombia, Venezuela, Mexico, and Panama were determined to see the plan succeed. Throughout 1983 and 1984, they continued their work, refining the treaty's terms and trying to persuade the nations of Central America to agree to it. A major breakthrough came in October 1984, when Nicaragua announced its intention of signing.

Then came a snag. Three countries, El Salvador, Honduras, and Costa Rica, suddenly shifted position. Although they had earlier supported Contadora, they now declared that they would not sign the treaty unless it was changed in several important ways. Leaders of the three nations conceded that they had changed their minds about signing at the urging of the United States.

Another Contadora snag developed the next

spring. In April 1985, Nicaraguan President Ortega visited the Soviet Union and other communist nations. He came away with a series of agreements aimed at helping Nicaragua solve its worsening economic problems. The agreements were a response to the Reagan administration's announcement, earlier in April, of new U.S. measures intended to further damage Nicaragua's economy. Ortega's move toward communism threatened the proposed treaty, the Contadora nations declared. So, they added, did the U.S. action that had prompted that move.

Why would this country fail to give wholehearted support to a plan to bring peace and democracy to Central America? One problem with the Contadora program, U.S. spokespersons said, was that, the way it would work out, U.S. military advisers in El Salvador and Honduras would be withdrawn before Cuban advisers left Nicaragua. Another was that the plan did not provide for a reliable way of making sure that Nicaragua was not shipping supplies and weapons to Salvadoran rebels. (In spite of the lack of independent evidence of such shipments, U.S. officials still maintained they were continuing.) A third U.S. objection to the Contadora plan was that it acknowledged the Sandinista government as the lawful government of Nicaragua. U.S. officials could not accept that.

But in the view of some, none of these was the real reason for U.S. reluctance to back Contadora. The ultimate reason, they said, had to do with another fundamental U.S. assumption about Latin America. This is the assumption that Latin America has become one of the great battlegrounds in a worldwide contest between democracy and totalitarianism, between capitalism and communism, between the United States and the Soviet Union — between "good" and "evil."

President Reagan and officials of his administration held this assumption as strongly as, perhaps more strongly than, officials of any other administration before them. Reagan considered the Soviet Union an "evil empire," and he frequently made clear his belief that the United States has a moral duty to do whatever it can to defeat this empire. On occasion, the president even hinted at a belief that the epic struggle between the United States and the Soviet Union might one day end in the Armageddon — final battle — of a nuclear conflagration.

Believing that Latin America may become the scene of one last clash between good and evil in the world, President Reagan found it difficult to favor any plan that might lead to compromise there. Approve a treaty that recognized the Sandinistas as the legitimate rulers of Nicaragua? Support a Colombian pact that acknowledged the rights of communists and the justice of some of their demands? Stop constructing military bases and preparing Central Americans for battle? Start encouraging President

Duarte to share power with leftists? How could any of these be right?

For their part, Latin Americans tended to see the situation in terms less black or white, less as a choice between utter evil and great good. In President Betancur's opinion, the either-or choice was "mad."

"I respect the right of states to work through their madness," he assured the United Nations in 1983. "But let them not seek Central America as the arena for their conflict."

The Colombian president also spoke of the Latin feeling of powerlessness in the face of superpower competition in their part of the world. "Violence, tensions, incidents, underdevelopment and injustice are all symptoms of a crisis in which coexistence and self-determination have been forgotten," he said. Superpower disregard for the rights of Latin America sees these powers "shamelessly interfering in lands where peasants leave their sowing to take up alien arms and to dig their own graves."

Must Latin Americans forever leave their fields to fight at the behest of others? Will U.S.-Soviet rivalry make compromise and coexistence impossible for them?

Many Latin Americans think it need not. Surely, they say, Latins are capable of acting to solve their own problems in their own way. The Duarte-Cienfuegos talks were a small step in that direction. So were the Colombian peace pacts. Contadora may yet turn out to be, they believe.

Latins know they bring certain strengths to their search for an end to injustice and unrest. The region has a flourishing academic community. Today more than ever, intellectuals throughout Latin America are trying to use their learning to find new ways of dealing with their ancient dilemmas. Even though Latin America's writers and scholars are often divided politically between right and left, most are sensitive to the need to shed the violent feudal past, and to enter fully into twentieth-century life and thought. "We are united by the concern over the great problems," says Mexican author Carlos Fuentes, "and we know that violence, repression, or terrorism cannot be resolved without rationality, adherence to law, popular support, imagination, knowledge of our past, and the bringing up to date of our culture."

Modern Latin America also has a host of committed democrats, and as 1985 began, there were stirrings of democracy in many nations. In Mexico, people were expressing concern about one-party politics and about the official laziness and corruption to which such politics have led. In El Salvador, a 1985 election to the nation's legislature saw voters turn away from both the extreme left and the extreme right in favor of candidates who shared President

Duarte's more moderate views. In Honduras, some military as well as some civilian leaders were growing restive about U.S. domination in their country. "People abroad [thought] that Honduras was a United States colony," one Honduran civilian politician complained. A military man sounded the same theme, not just for Honduras, but for all Central America. "The United States thinks . . . of us as controlled countries." The Hondurans, like President Betancur of Colombia, hope the United States will allow Latin Americans to choose their own paths for the future.

In Argentina, in 1985, a freely elected president, Raúl Alfonsín, was striving to lead his country in democratic ways. Argentina has had only seven years of democratic rule over the last half-century. Like Duarte in El Salvador, Alfonsín was obviously going to find it tough to establish traditions of political freedom among people to whom such traditions are unfamiliar. But many Argentines were optimistic about his chances. Optimism was also growing in Uruguay and Brazil in the mid-1980s, as military dictators in both nations were replaced by civilian leaders. Even Chile's General Pinochet was seeing unrest grow almost daily late in 1984. And, of course, Latin America already had several working democracies: Colombia, Venezuela, Belize, Costa Rica.

Another instrument of change in Latin America seems likely to be the Roman Catholic Church. After centuries of standing for conservatism and authoritarian government, the Church is modifying its position. A few priests have joined left-wing movements. "Christ led me to Marx," says a Nicaraguan priest named Ernesto Cardenál. "I'm a Marxist who believes in God, follows Christ, and is a revolutionary for the sake of His kingdom."

The Catholic Church officially condemns such radical "liberation theology," saying it leads to resentment and fighting between rich and poor. Yet even moderate Catholic leaders are taking a more active role in seeking social justice for Latin America. Salvadoran Church officials, for instance, negotiate between leftists and the government. In 1984, they arranged for several exchanges of prisoners. "The Church is the channel with the most credibility" in El Salvador, says the nation's auxiliary bishop, Gregorio Rosa Chávez.

In Chile, and in some other countries, the Church has taken responsibility for providing refuge for the poor and for those persecuted by the government. Priests and nuns attempt to take the anger and the hostility they find on the streets and in the slums and turn it to peaceful, constructive uses. "The role of organized groups is crucial these days, especially if they have leaders committed to nonviolence," according to one Chilean priest. "Otherwise it will be difficult to channel the hatred and rancor that people are feeling."

Other resources for Latin America's would-be reformers lie outside their own borders. Modern transportation and communication make it more possible than before for Latins to find support from the peoples of other lands. And not just from the United States and the Soviet Union, either. They can look to Japan or to the People's Republic of China. They can look to the democracies of Western Europe. In 1984, the leaders of a group of Western European nations meeting in Costa Rica promised to double their economic assistance to Central America. In making that commitment, the groups overrode U.S. objections to including help for Nicaragua in their plan.

One European nation with a particular interest in offering aid to Latin America was Spain. In February 1984, that nation announced its intention of sending a "mini Peace Corps" to Central America. Like the members of the Peace Corps established by President Kennedy in the early 1960s, the one hundred Spanish volunteers planned to work to improve health care, to set up cooperatives to help farmers and artisans sell their wares, and to assist government administrators in handling such matters as traffic problems and sewage disposal. "It makes sense for us to spend . . . money for aid . . . in Latin America," one Spanish official said. "We have blood ties and historical ties with these people. They are our brothers."

Spain's prime minister, Felipe González Márquez, offered his own personal help to his brothers and sisters as well. González, a socialist, became prime minister in 1982. He governs under a democratic constitution adopted by Spain in the 1970s. Like President Betancur of Colombia, González wanted to mediate among the nations of Central America and help them to live together in peace.

González also indicated his desire to see democracy and civil rights strengthened in Latin America. He wanted to see them strengthened quickly, too, in time for the five hundredth anniversary of Columbus's discovery of the New World. By October 12, 1992, González said in 1984, there should be not "one single Spanish-speaking citizen who could not affirm that he lives in freedom."

Is González's too wild a dream? Too bright a hope? Many, seeing Latin America's problems and recognizing U.S. and Soviet determination to play superpower politics there, feared it was. Yet others were resolved to cling to his vision. Latin America has suffered, as Simón Bolívar predicted it would, so much torment in the name of freedom. Isn't it time, at last, for freedom itself?

Selected Bibliography

In doing research for *Good Neighbors? The United States and Latin America,* I referred to the books listed below for background information about the history and culture of the area. Current events information in chapter 1, and in chapters 5 through 9, came from newspapers and news magazines, and from the publications of the three organizations whose names and addresses follow the bibliography.

Collier, Simon. *From Cortes to Castro: An Introduction to the History of Latin America, 1492–1973.* New York: Macmillan, 1974.

Connell-Smith, Gordon. *The United States and Latin America: An Historical Analysis of Inter-American Relations.* New York: John Wiley & Sons, 1974.

Fagg, John Edwin. *Latin America: A General History.* New York: Macmillan, 1963.

Meyer, Karl E., and Tad Szulc. *The Cuban Invasion: The Chronicle of Disaster.* New York: Praeger, 1962.

Rothchild, John, ed. *Latin America Yesterday and Today.* New York: Bantam Books, 1973.

Skidmore, Thomas E., and Peter H. Smith. *Modern Latin America.* New York: Oxford University Press, 1984.

Williams, Byron. *Cuba: The Continuing Revolution.* New York: Parents' Magazine Press, 1969.

Center for Defense Information
303 Capitol Gallery West
600 Maryland Avenue, S.W.
Washington, D.C. 20024

Common Cause
2030 M Street, N.W.
Washington, D.C. 20036

Federation of American Scientists
307 Massachusetts Avenue, N.E.
Washington, D.C. 20002

Spanish and Portuguese Words Used in This Book

Barrio suburbano — suburb. Used ironically to mean a slum. (Sp.)

Cabildo — town council. (Sp.)

Callampa — mushroom. A slum. (Sp.)

Caudillo — strong man, dictator. (Sp.)

Colono — laborer. (Sp.)

Conquistador — conqueror. (Sp.)

Contra — against. Rebel fighting against Nicaragua's Sandinista government. (Sp.)

Cortes/côrtes — local representative assemblies that developed in medieval Spain and Portugal. (*cortes,* Sp.; *côrtes,* Port.)

Criollo — creole. In colonial times, a person of European parents or ancestry who lived his or her life in the Americas. In modern times, the word is generally used to include persons of mixed white, black, and Indian ancestry. (Sp.)

Desaparecidos — disappeared ones. Victims of Latin American death squads. (Sp.)

Encomienda — labor system under which American Indians worked as near-slaves for their European masters. (Sp.)

Favela — slum. (Port.)

Fazenda — large estate. (Port.)

Junta — governing committee. (Sp.)

Hacienda — large estate. (Sp.)

Mestizo — person of mixed (European and Indian) parentage or ancestry. (Sp.)

Peninsulare — peninsular. In colonial times, a European who governed in the New World, then returned to his homeland. Also, a member of his family. (Sp.)

Pueblo joven — new town. A slum. (Sp.)

Turba — from *turbar,* to disturb or alarm. Member of a Sandinista death squad. (Sp.)

Index